I had the feeling Jackie was chattering more than usual because she was nervous. The thought made me feel more at ease.

"I wouldn't have thought your parents would have let you come by yourself. That stretch of the road through the woods is sort of lonesome," my dad said.

"Well, actually I'm pretty independent," Jackie said. Her smile faded a little. "They don't worry about me too much."

I rushed to her rescue. "The woods aren't so bad in the daytime. It's only after dark that some people think they get kind of spooky."

"I can understand that," Jackie said.

"When you get ready to leave, Shane will ride out to the other side of the woods with you. Okay, Shane?" There was no arguing with Dad when he used that tone of voice. Even Jackie recognized that.

"Shane knows the woods like the back of his hand," Dad said. The note of pride in his voice surprised me.

Dear Readers:

In our last letter we told you about *Journey's End*, the first of Becky Stuart's series featuring Kellogg, Carey and Kellogg's faithful dog, Theodore. In book #2, *Someone Else*, to be published in February, the famous trio solves another mystery: just where has Carey's neighbor gone? Theodore is the first to know, and you may be sure the answer is a surprise to all concerned.

Now we would like to call your attention to *Orinoco Adventure*, scheduled for January, Elaine Harper's first Romantic Adventure. Romantic Adventures are Blossom Valley Books that are not set in Blossom Valley. Each one will have a map so that you may follow for yourself the travels of the characters. Look for the words Romantic Adventure on the front cover, under the Blossom Valley arch. You'll be glad you did!

Nancy Jackson
Senior Editor
FIRST LOVE FROM SILHOUETTE

A CHANCE HERO
Ann Gabhart

First Love from Silhouette

Published by Silhouette Books New York

America's Publisher of Contemporary Romance

SILHOUETTE BOOKS
300 E. 42nd St., New York, N.Y. 10017

Copyright © 1985 by Ann Gabhart

Distributed by Pocket Books

All rights reserved, including the right to reproduce
this book or portions thereof in any form whatsoever.
For information address Silhouette Books,
300 E. 42nd St., New York, N.Y. 10017

ISBN: 0-373-06161-7

First Silhouette Books printing November 1985

10 9 8 7 6 5 4 3 2 1

All the characters in this book are fictitious. Any resemblance to actual persons, living or dead, is purely coincidental.

SILHOUETTE, FIRST LOVE FROM SILHOUETTE and
colophon are registered trademarks of the publisher.

America's Publisher of Contemporary Romance

Printed in the U.S.A.

RL 4.3, IL Age 10 and up

ANN GABHART was born and brought up in Kentucky where she still lives. A real country girl, she is most happy when she is outdoors amid living and growing things. She began her very first book at the age of ten and has been writing ever since. Her three children have grown up to the sound of her typewriter clacking. Among her interests are reading, word games and basketball.

Chapter One

The light of the sun dimmed when we entered the woods. Hickories, oaks and maples pushed in on the road from both sides until it seemed there wouldn't be room for the big yellow bus to weave its way through. But Mr. Smithers never slowed down. I was the only kid on the bus. I'm first on in the morning and last off in the afternoon. Mr. Smithers says that's what I get for living in the middle of Chance Woods.

I searched the woods going by with my eyes while I half listened to Mr. Smithers chattering. Every once in a while I nodded my head. It's not that I don't like Mr. Smithers—I do. He tells some great stories about the woods, but some days, when things haven't gone so smoothly at school, I need to drink in the sight of the trees.

The bus scooted out into the clearing, and Mr. Smithers jerked it to a stop with a screech of the brakes like always. "Well, kid, we made it through one more time. 'Course, now I got to go back through by myself."

"You'll make it," I said solemnly. "The trees will hold back their branches and let you pass."

"There's been times when they didn't, and it didn't take but once for me to learn to carry that." Mr. Smithers pointed at the shiny ax propped between the heater and the dashboard. "Let me tell you, it's a long and lonesome walk back to civilization out of Chance Woods."

I smiled, probably for the first time all day. Aunt Jo tells me that if I'd smile more all the girls would be after me, but I doubt it. I stopped next to Mr. Smithers and said, "What are you going to do if a tree bigger than you can chop through falls in the road?" We've had this very same conversation at least a hundred times until by now it seems almost a ritual to go through the whole story.

Mr. Smithers laughed and slapped his leg. "Well, at least I'll have my ax for protection." Suddenly he was serious again. "There's strange things in Chance Woods, Shane, my boy, and don't you ever forget it."

"You mean bears, Mr. Smithers?"

"I ain't saying exactly what kind of creatures, but they're not the kind you would want to meet up with face-to-face without some kind of weapon."

Mr. Smithers is in his sixties, several pounds too heavy, and with a wheeze from smoking too much. The thought of him fighting off a bear, much less some kind of strange creature, made me want to smile again, but I didn't. I just said, "Well, good luck getting home."

"Yeah, kid, and good luck to you tonight in your game. This is the last one of the season, ain't it?"

"Yeah."

"I've been aiming to come all year to see you play. Maybe I'll come out tonight."

"I don't get up to bat much. Mostly I just collect splinters, but it ought to be a pretty good game tonight. Willie's pitching."

"Yeah, Willie. He's that kid who used to give me trouble on the bus, always throwing paper wads or something. When he turned sixteen, I sent his folks a contribution to help buy him a car."

"Now he's throwing fast balls and giving the other teams trouble. Willie's our best player. The hero of the team."

"Maybe it'll be your turn to be the hero tonight, kid," Mr. Smithers said before he cranked the door shut.

I just shook my head and waved after Mr. Smithers turned the bus around and headed back through the woods. It wasn't ever going to be my turn to be the hero. Not in baseball, anyway. Not like Willie. Willie's tall and a little lanky, but with plenty of muscles, too. He can throw a fast ball that nobody can hit and then get up to bat and pound one over the fence. But he's not a one-sport man. Come basketball season, and then he's into hook shots and fast breaks. He's the kind of all-around athlete that my dad was in high school and that I was supposed to be.

But somewhere along the line, my legs forgot to get any longer. I've been stuck at five foot five forever. Sometimes I think I've been that size all my life until I remember playing Little League ball, when everybody else was five five and I had to stand on a box to be five foot. But it's not just my size. When I grip a ball to throw it, my fingers take on a mind of their own and spring out in all the wrong directions, no matter how many times Dad shows me the right way to hold my hand.

Dad's always been patient with me. He'll work with me for hours until I know every technique in the book. The trouble is I can never get it to work for me. I know how, but knowing and doing are two different things. But you've got to hand it to Dad. He never gives up, not even when I wish, even pray, that he would.

Dad used to be a coach. I wish he still was, because the truth is he's a great teacher and it's a shame that it's all wasted on me. He took his football team over in Whitesburg to the finals one year. They said he probably would have won the championship the next year, but then my mom died and Dad quit coaching, and we moved here right in the middle of Chance Woods when I was ten years old.

So for five years I've been Dad's only prospect, and for five years I've failed about as miserably as anybody can fail. But like I said, you've got to give Dad credit. He won't let me give up.

The lane to our house from the main road winds through the woods for about a half mile. A wide pasture has been cleared on each side of the lane, and the trees have to keep their distance. Each year they try to edge nearer to to one another, but I cut them back. We've got a few cows who keep the grass down in the summer, but Dad doesn't actually farm. He's a salesman now. Textbooks and such. I guess he's good at it. But then he's good at everything he tries.

As I came up over the little rise where I could finally see the two-story white house nestled in a cluster of sugar maples, I hoped against hope that Dad's gray station wagon wouldn't be pulled up in front of the house, but it was. No matter how late Dad might be on other nights, he always made it home in time for my games. I knew he would be sitting at the kitchen table. He'd be drinking coffee and filling out his sales records for the day while he waited for me to get home so we could pass a few balls and warm up for the game. You'd think after all these years he'd know that sitting in school all day was all the warm-up I needed.

I glanced across the field at the woods. A breeze ruffled the spring-fresh leaves on the trees until they seemed to be whispering to me to come. I did, most days. I'd just prop my books up in the crook of the old apple tree that kept vigil in the middle of the pasture and disappear into the woods for an hour or two. Of course, Dad wasn't usually home, and I didn't have a baseball game to get to.

The thought of the game made the depths of the woods look even more inviting. As if on cue, my dog Maybe bounded out of the woods and halfway across the field before he stopped and cocked his head at me.

Ever since we got him, we've been trying to figure out exactly which breeds you'd have to mix to come up with Maybe. As a matter of fact, that's how he got his name. The man who gave him to us said that Maybe was part collie or maybe part retriever and maybe part hound. Maybe he'd get big, and maybe he wouldn't. About the only thing old Mr. Jeffries admitted to being sure about was that Maybe was a dog and sort of brown.

That's about all we're sure about even now. He's gotten big enough, growing in leaps and bounds until now he's this overgrown creature with medium-length dark brown fur that draws cockleburs. He's not much of a tracker or a watch dog, but he's got a heart as big as Chance Woods.

I looked from Maybe to the house and sighed before I called to him. "Sorry old boy, but not today."

Usually when I walk on toward the house, Maybe drops his ears and joins me with this resigned look. But not this time. He barked at me three times before he loped back into the woods. So instead, my shoulders drooped as I moved on toward the house. At least this was the last game and school would be out soon. Then I'd have whole days to explore the woods. Days of being alone where I could forget girls and sports. Seemed like lately both were equally bewildering to me. Trouble was that while I could happily never see a baseball again, I didn't feel the same about girls. I wanted them to like me. Especially Tami.

I was halfway down the hill, kicking rocks in front of me to slow me down, when Maybe's frantic barking stopped me. Turtles are about the biggest game Maybe ever corners. That might be because turtles are the only animals in existence that don't have time to get away when they hear Maybe crashing through the trees. But this wasn't Maybe's familiar turtle bark.

Through the trees his barking hit a new high note, a note I'd never heard before. I dropped my books on the ground and ran for the woods. When a friend hollers like that, you go see what he's found, baseball game or no baseball game.

I found a break in the underbrush and pushed my way into the woods. Chance Woods is a wilderness of trees that covers acres and acres. Nobody really knows how many. Old Mr. Chance, who used to own it all, died years ago, but even before he died he'd let the place go wild, only keeping clear the little bit we live on now. That's all we own. The rest belongs to the old man's two nieces, who used to live in Chicago. At least, they did when we bought the house from them. Nobody seems to know where they are now, and so the woods just sits here growing wilder by the year.

The local people say there's more than one reason why it's called Chance Woods. There are plenty who say you're taking a chance just walking into the woods, and not many venture into its depths. The folks about tell their kids all kinds of stories about people who wandered in and were never seen or heard from again. Mr. Smithers has told me more than a few of them, but I don't know how much of it all to believe. Stories like that have a way of getting exaggerated.

Once through the underbrush, I stopped to listen and get my bearings. Maybe's barking was even more frenzied than before and growing more distant. I began to run, zigzagging between the trees and hopping over downed branches.

Up ahead of me, Maybe had stopped and was barking in a circle now. His high-pitched yaps were getting closer when I miscalculated a fallen tree and caught my toe in one of the branches. I fell flat on my face in a cushion of leaves. As I lay there struggling to get my breath, there was one more bark from Maybe, followed by a yelp of pain. All I could think of as I scrambled to my feet was that Maybe had cornered a rabid fox or skunk. And I couldn't remember how long it had been since he'd gotten his rabies shot.

Then I smelled about the worst smell in the world. I thought skunk again, but this wasn't exactly the odor of a skunk. It was more like something very dead, but if that was so Maybe would just have rolled around on the carcass and come on home. Even he knew that dead animals didn't need treeing.

"Maybe!" I yelled as I stood there not sure exactly which direction I should take. There was nothing but quiet now, the kind of silence that is louder than a million noises. Not a bird called and not an insect hummed. It was so quiet I could hear the tree beside me flutter its leaves.

There was a great crashing sound as something began moving through the trees again. As I ran toward the sound, I thought Maybe was outdoing himself to be able to make that much noise. Still, it was a relief to hear the noise, for surely that meant he hadn't been hurt too badly in whatever encounter he'd had. But there wasn't any more barking.

I never even saw Maybe come out of the trees in front of me. A hump of brown fur was just there cowering at my feet, and from the depths of the woods the noise of something moving through the trees got farther and farther away until there was only the distant rustle of brush.

I dropped to my knees beside Maybe and ran my hands over his back and legs. I couldn't find anything wrong with him except that he looked like about the most done-in dog you might ever want to see. His ears were plastered against his head. His eyes were wide and shining like glass. His sides were heaving as he panted in quick, short bursts. I'd seen dogs scared of storms who looked like that, but Maybe, in his ignorance, had never been afraid of anything. That is until now, and just looking at him, I felt a little quiver of fear. At the same time, I wanted to take out after whatever it was and see for myself if there really were strange creatures in the woods like Mr. Smithers said, or if it was a bear. After all, any dog in his right mind would be scared of a bear.

But I'd already been in the woods at least twenty minutes, and Dad was going to be fit to be tied as it was. We found the shortest route out, and Maybe was glad enough to go. He kept his nose practically against my leg as he limped along behind me. He wouldn't raise his ears away from his head, though I stopped and ruffled his fur and talked to him a dozen times before we hit the sunshine of the pasture.

By then my ears were laid back a little too, because I could see Dad on the porch waiting for me.

"Was the game canceled?" he asked when I came into the yard.

"No, sir, but there's an hour to go before I have to be there." I looked toward him, but I kept my eyes away from his. He was mad. I could tell that without seeing his gray eyes narrow at me. It was the way he stood, as if he had planted his feet and was ready for a tackle.

"That doesn't give us time to warm up."

I dropped my head. "I'm sorry, Dad, but Maybe treed something in the woods."

"What? A turtle?" Dad's voice was flat and angry.

"No, this was something big, and it hurt him. Look at him, Dad," I pleaded, finally daring to look at his face. "He looks as if he's seen the devil himself."

Dad tightened his mouth as if forcing the words he wanted to say to stay inside. After staring at me for another long moment, he let out a long sigh and turned to Maybe. "What's the matter with him?"

"I'm not sure. He's limping, but I couldn't find any marks on him."

Dad squatted next to Maybe, who was sitting at my feet still the very picture of terror. Dad probed Maybe's haunches and said, "Looks like he had a scare, all right. That must have been some big turtle, Maybe, old boy."

"Do you think he's hurt? I mean, he's just not scared. I heard him yelp when whatever it was hit him."

"You heard him yelp—you don't know that anything hit him," Dad said as he stood up. "I think he's okay."

"Something was there. Do you think it could have been a bear?"

A frown tightened Dad's forehead, and a look settled in his eyes that he always gets when he thinks I'm making something up. He doesn't like pretending. He never has. He wants everything in black and white, sure, and backed by visible facts. "No, I don't think it could have been a bear. You're letting your imagination run away with you again."

"Yeah, I guess you're right." I ruffled Maybe's ears one more time. They were beginning to lift away from his head, and his eyes, though they were still wary, weren't quite so glazed with fright.

Dad reached over and punched my shoulder. "He'll be all right, Shane. Maybe's a tough dog. Now, we haven't got much time. You'd better get ready."

As I turned to go into the huose, he followed me and said, "It could be you'll do better without so much warming up. You won't be tired out before the game. I remember once I was late to a baseball game. The coach wouldn't let me play the first three innings, and then before I went in all the warm-up I had was throwing a little on the sideline. I hit two over the fence that day."

Dad's always finding a reason to hope that *this* game things would be different. This game I'll get to play. This game I'll hit the ball or catch it or do something. It would be funny if it didn't mean so much to him.

Dad gave me his before-game pep talk all the way into town and out to the school. I tried to listen, but I kept remembering the sound of Maybe's "big turtle" crashing through the trees and wondering what it was.

When Dad pulled up to let me off in front of the locker room, he said, "Remember now, the most important thing is to concentrate. If you can concentrate your whole body on something and believe you can do it, you can."

I nodded just as if he hadn't said the same thing to me at least a thousand times and as if I really thought I'd get off the bench and have a chance to try out his theory. I wondered how many games I'd started with those words ringing in my ears. I used to believe it. I was sure that if I just concentrated enough I could make the bat hit the ball over the fence. But I could never concentrate enough, and after a while I couldn't believe enough either.

When we went out to the field, Tami Collins was the first person I saw as I glanced over the small crowd in the bleachers. Tami just sort of jumps out and grabs your attention whether she's trying to or not, and I was smart enough to know that she wasn't trying to get my attention. It's a natural thing with her. She's pretty, sort of tall and slender in the right places and not so slender in the other right places, with long, curly blond hair that blows back in the wind like a model's in a magazine ad. She has a cute little smile and eyes that are as blue as mine but not so dark.

Everybody has always told me I have nice eyes. Aunt Jo tells me that at least three times every time I see her. I guess she thinks that will boost my confidence in how I look. People used to tell me my eyes were like my mother's, but of course nobody here ever knew my mother except Aunt Jo, and she and Dad don't talk about her.

Willie went over to the fence, and Tami smiled at him and called out, "Good luck." I held my breath as I watched for his reaction. If Willie was after her, I'd never stand a chance of being noticed. But he just grinned and waved a little before he ran out onto the field to get warmed up. Willie's one of those guys who hasn't got a lot of time for girls. Sports are the important thing for him. Especially baseball. He's hoping to be scouted by the big leagues before he graduates next year. The more I think about it the more I know Willie and Dad were made for each other, and I wonder if maybe there was a mix-up at the hospital. But then Willie's older than me, already turned sixteen.

Me, I've always liked girls. It's just getting them to like me that gives me problems. Maybe I should say it's just even letting them know I'm alive that gives me trouble. It's easier for me to admire them from a distance like I'd been doing with Tami.

I almost worked up enough nerve to go over and pick up a bat by the fence right in front of where she was sitting, but I hesitated too long. The coach hollered something, and the umpire yelled, "Play ball!"

The game went pretty fast. I was keeping a record of the other pitcher's throws. Like I said, I know baseball. I just can't translate my knowledge into action. We were one run up in the next-to-the-last inning when Coach Wyatt motioned down at the end of the bench at me. I actually looked around to see who he wanted, but I was the only one there.

I hustled up to him with my record of pitches. "Odds are he's going to throw a fast ball to the inside unless he loses it, and then it'll go high," I said quickly.

The coach looked suitably impressed. "You think so, kid?"

"I said odds are."

The coach stood up and made a couple of signs over at the third-base coach. He came back and sat down beside me. "If it's a sinker for a strike, our goose is cooked now."

"It won't be a sinker," I said. Confidence was easy when it was all calculated on paper.

"But that wasn't why I called you over here," the coach said and then fell quiet. Every fiber in his body was concentrated on Bobby Smott, who was batting. Talking with the coach was like that, only a few words between pitches no matter which side was in town, but he never lost his place in the conversation.

The pitch was a ball, high. Bobby drew a walk. "Way to call them, kid," the coach said. "We could use another couple of runs."

"We've got a chance at it. I think their pitcher's getting tired."

"Yeah, well, we're a run up even if we don't score this inning. All we've got to do is hold them in the top of the ninth." The coach paused as if considering something. Then he called Red Jones back from the on-deck circle where he'd been doctoring his bat.

Red's a pretty good hitter. Not great, but he usually comes through in the clutch situations. So I was surprised the coach was calling him back. There were already two outs, and this was maybe our last shot at some extra runs. But you don't question the coach. That's one of the first rules I ever learned.

The coach looked at me and said, "Get your bat, kid. You're pinch-hitting for Red."

You could have knocked me off the bench with a feather. Me pinch-hitting for Red was the craziest thing I'd ever heard, and I broke the first rule. "You sure, Coach?"

"What do you think, kid? Get in there and knock 'em dead."

I wanted to refuse. I just wanted to go back down to the end of the bench and sit there quietly until the last hurrah was over. Instead I shrugged and said, "You're the coach."

It felt funny picking up a bat and walking out to the batter's box. I knew enough to stop halfway and do some stretching. I also needed the time to give my stomach orders not to get sick.

My eyes raked across the crowd as I swung the bat a few times. Everywhere heads were leaning together as people tried to figure out what the coach was doing or even who I was. I knew what Coach Wyatt was doing. He was trying to be nice, since he figured this would be my last chance to get up to bat. I felt like going over and giving him a lesson in coaching. Coaches weren't supposed to be nice. They were supposed to go for blood all the time. I mean, winning was the name of the game, and I felt a little sicker when I thought that the other team might come back in the next inning and make a couple of runs to beat us. The coach would never forgive me for inspiring such a foolish, kindhearted deed in him.

I picked up a handful of dust and made mud with the sweat in my palms. I rubbed it off on my pants and walked toward the plate. I couldn't put it off forever.

A voice called from the bleachers, "We need a hit, Shane. You can do it."

I didn't have to look around to know it was Tami, and she'd known my name. I sneaked a peek over my shoulder at her as I dug the required hole in the batter's box. A few of the others in the crowd had taken up the chatter and were hollering encouragement to me. But my father was sitting like always. He was a little off to the side and not moving. You would have never known this was my first time at bat all year. I had pinch-run a few times because I'm good at reading the other team's signs and the coach likes to get me on second. But now Dad's eyes were concentrated on me, and I felt as if every bit of his energy was coiled up like a fist in my stomach.

He really thought I could do it. I wondered if maybe it wouldn't be better just to get sick right there on homeplate than to let him down again. I mean, the coach was being nice, but he expected me to make an out. The crowd was puzzled but was willing to wait until I struck out before they hissed, but Dad really thought I could hit the ball. The far end of the bench had never looked so good.

The first pitch was by me and the umpire was calling "Strike one" before I was ready to swing. Bad concentration, I could hear my father whispering in my ear. Bad concentration. Two balls that were close enough to make a batter sweat and another strike later and I had yet to swing.

"Come on, kid. Swing the bat," the coached yelled from the dugout. As far as I could remember, that was the first time all year that the coach had yelled out at anybody while they were batting. He was always yelling at or for them mentally or sending them signs, but these were words yelled out loud. Words I couldn't ignore. He'd sent me up to the plate to swing.

I started watching the next ball before it left the pitcher's hand. It was a sinker right over the middle of the plate. I knew that as soon as he turned it loose. I pulled back my bat and swung. It was a great swing, perfect in every way, and I had called the pitch right, but I was just a little high with my bat. I sort of killed the ball right down to the ground, where it died about three feet out in front of the plate with a dull thud.

I dropped the bat and raced for first base. It wouldn't have been a bad bunt if I'd been trying to bunt, but I still would have been out if the other team hadn't decided to help me. The pitcher and catcher collided as they scrambled after the ball, and I was safe at first. Then Bobby, who was dancing off second, drew a throw that went out into center field. He raced toward home, and I headed to second.

The guy in center field didn't chance throwing the ball. He ran it all the way in with his eyes on me like I was a real threat to go. I decided if Bobby could do it, so could I. I danced off second, weaving first one way and then another. I was on the wrong side of my weave when the fielder finally shot the ball in. My belly-down flop in the dirt didn't confuse the umpire for a minute. I was out.

I got up, hit at the dust on my uniform, and followed the other team off the field. I didn't look at Dad, but the crowd was cheering in a general sort of way.

The coach clapped me on the back. I'd made the out he'd expected me to make, but we had gotten a run out of it. He hadn't expected that. "Way to go, Buckley," he said. "But shooting for three errors on the same play was a little cheeky."

"I'm sorry, Coach, I didn't aim to get so far off base."

But the coach had already turned away and was sending in a new fielder for Red, and I was making my way to the end of the bench. It was as familiar and comfortable as an unmade bed. When I finally looked up at Dad, he was sitting there exactly the same, with no expression on his face.

Chapter Two

Coach Wyatt kept us a long time in the locker room with his last-game-of-the-season speech about how everybody on the team had made a contribution and how much he had enjoyed working with us. Coaches always say the same things, from Little League on up.

I didn't really listen. I'd heard it all lots of times before, and none of it had ever applied to me. The only reason I even made the team was because of my dad. Coaches have a lot of respect for each other. Instead I thought first about Tami and how she had called me by name and then about the strange, heavy thing crashing through the woods. I didn't know which thought intrigued me more.

Finally the coach went around the room and shook everybody's hand. Since we had won by one run, I could tell he was glad he'd let himself be moved to do me a favor. He had a sort of pleased glow about him, and I knew that forever more he'd like me even though it was actually the other team's errors that had given us the run we needed.

Outside it was already night. Parents were in their cars waiting. Under the light outside the door, Tami stood in the middle of a giggling huddle of girls who were waiting to congratulate the team. There must have been four or five girls there, but Tami gathered all the light to herself and all the eyes. The other girls were just backup.

I had to walk right past them to get to the car. I practiced saying "Hi, Tami" over and over in my head. After all, she knew my name. I couldn't pass by without speaking even if sweat from my armpits was trickling down my sides and my heart was hammering worse than it had when I went up to bat.

"Hi, Tami," I managed to spit out a little too eagerly when I got close enough.

Her eyes looked past me on to the other team members straggling out of the locker room even as she said, "Oh, hi, Shane. That was the funniest hit I've seen all year."

Then she giggled a little and, seeing Willie come out the door, she ran down the walk toward him. No girl would ever run down the walk to congratulate me on my great game. That was for the heroes, not the clowns. I looked back over my shoulder at her and felt a great hopelessness settle inside me as I headed reluctantly for the car. It was never fun riding home with

Dad after a game even when I didn't get into the action.

"You got the run in," a girl's voice said beside me. "That was the important thing. If you hadn't swung, then you'd have probably been out and nothing would have happened—the game would be tied and we'd still be out there trying to win."

I looked around at Jackie Adams. I knew Jackie, of course. Any admirer of Tami's would have to know Jackie. She was like Tami's shadow, a little slimmer and taller, with long, dark hair and hazel eyes that I couldn't see right now. I could see her smile, and I knew she was sincere in what she was saying.

"Thanks, Jackie. But I guess it was pretty funny."

"Don't mind Tami," Jackie said. "She hasn't got eyes for anybody but Willie right now. She'll get over it."

I looked at Jackie curiously, trying to really see her in the dim light. "Why should she get over it? Willie's a great guy."

"Sure," she said as if she wasn't all sure. She stepped back away from me a little bit.

I didn't know exactly what to do next. I was torn between wanting to hang around till maybe Tami came back and making a fast exit before I said something really dumb. After an awkward silence, I hunched my shoulders and said, "See you around."

Jackie surprised me again. "We have lunch period at the same time. Come sit by me sometime."

"Yeah, sure." I hadn't noticed her during lunch break. I knew Tami had lunch break after me because I always passed her in the hall as I went back to class.

Dad was quiet most of the miles home, and I thought maybe I was going to get off the hook and not have to listen to a play-by-play critique of each player's good and bad moves. I wished he could just be happy that I had, as Jackie said, knocked in the run because I wasn't afraid to swing and let it go at that, but he couldn't.

When we turned off the highway onto Chance Road, which winds its way back through the trees to home, he said, "If you think I'm going to congratulate you on that comedy of errors that they let pass as a hit, you're wrong."

I clamped down on the sigh that welled up inside me. "I'm sorry, Dad. I just didn't get my bat on it good."

He didn't say anything. I tried just to let the silence run on, but it was so heavy in the car I felt as if it was mashing me. So I said, "We won the game."

"It isn't winning that's important. It's doing your personal best."

That was my personal best, I wanted to yell at him, but I didn't. Instead I said, "Coach Wyatt wasn't mad."

"He shouldn't even have put you up at a time like that. He could have lost the game."

"But we didn't."

"It wasn't a great season by any standard," Dad growled. "Six and five."

"A winning season."

The silence sprouted up in the car again. I wasn't content to let it grow. "I heard a rumor at school today. They say Coach Bingham got a job coaching down in Florida next year. I guess that means the job of football coach will be open."

"So?" Dad's voice carried a warning, but I ignored it.

"So I thought you might want to apply. You could make the team into something."

"I'm through coaching," Dad said flatly.

If only he was, I thought, not wanting to look into the future to see which sport he would start pushing me toward next. He was right about my hit. It was a comedy of errors. My whole athletic career, if you could call it that, had been a comedy of errors. There was the time in Little League when I had swung so hard and missed that I fell down and sprained my ankle. At least I was out for the rest of the season. Then in junior pro football one year I had actually caught a pass and would have made a touchdown too, if one of my own teammates hadn't caught me and tackled me on our own five-yard line. Last but not least in humiliation was the time in junior high when the coach put me in the game with one second showing on the clock. I held up the game for five minutes checking in, just so I could stand on the floor while the buzzer sounded. I'd never been the hero, but I'd always been the clown.

Thinking about all those embarrassing moments steeled me for Dad's anger as I said, "What happened over at Whitesburg that made you give up coaching?" I'd always been curious, but I'd never had the nerve to ask.

Dad answered me, but his voice was low and tight. "I just got tired of it, that's all."

I wanted to call him on the obvious lie, but there are times it's best to let the silence grow. Besides, we were getting into the woods now. The moon was bright, and I might see something at night that I'd never see in daylight.

We were almost home when my eyes caught on a large, bulky shadow just inside the tree line. I thought it was just a bush taking on new dimensions in the moonlight until the lights hit it and two spots of red glittered out of the top of the shadow.

"Look, Dad. There's something strange there in the woods."

He pulled off to the side, braked to a stop and looked in the direction I was pointing. "I don't see anything."

And I didn't either. Not then. Whatever it was had disappeared. I'd kept my eyes on it, and I'd swear it hadn't moved. But even so it was gone. "It's not there now," I admitted.

Dad didn't start the car up for a few minutes. He gripped the wheel and stared straight ahead. He wouldn't even look toward the woods again, but I kept my eyes trained on the trees. Whatever it was might pop back into sight.

Dad's voice was so strange when he spoke again that I thought for a minute he had turned the radio on. "There's nothing there, Shane. It was your imagination."

"But Dad, I saw it."

"You saw it in your mind. Only in your own mind. You're too much like Linda."

My eyes came away from the woods then and back to Dad. Linda was my mother, but Dad never talked about her. Lots of times I wanted to talk about her, but whenever I would ask something about her, Dad would frown with that certain dark worry in his eyes and shut the memories away. Aunt Jo said it was because remembering hurt him so much, but she wouldn't talk about my mother either. Now Dad had brought her name out into the dark between us himself.

"How?" I said, not sure I should ask.

"She was afraid of things that weren't there." Dad's voice was tired and hollow sounding, as if he were speaking from the end of a long tunnel.

"I'm not afraid," I insisted. It seemed important that he believe me. "And it was there. I saw it."

"She was always sure, too," he said. He shifted the car back into gear and pulled back onto the road.

I couldn't say anything more. The words stuck in my throat. I'd never seen Dad like this. He was usually so sure, so confident, so ready for any kind of challenge. I didn't look back at the woods. Instead I stared straight ahead at the road, not wanting to see any more glowing red eyes or shadowy shapes that disappeared without a trace.

The special pain of remembering my mom settled around my heart. I had loved her so much. Before she got sick, she had played with me, sung to me, devoted hours of her time to me while Dad was at practice. And she had had a fantastic imagination. Together we played pretend games that sometimes went on for days. Games we kept secret from Dad. That pretending had been fun, like reading a storybook and becoming one of the characters in your mind.

I don't remember much about her illness except that she went away from me and I didn't know what to do. After she died, I tried to wish her back into being. I pretended then like I've never pretended before or since, but it didn't work. All that my dreaming and pretending did was upset Dad.

The fun of pretending died with my mother, and now the only time I pretend is when I practice sports with my dad. It hadn't been only my imagination. I really had seen the shape of some kind of large animal. Maybe it was a bear standing upright; the glittering eyes had been high in the air.

I dared a glance over at Dad. I wanted to say something to make him believe me, but no words came to mind. I let the silence keep growing between us.

It was the next morning before it was broken. Dad woke me up early. "I've got to go to the city to turn in my sales reports."

I raised myself up on my elbow and nodded. There was something heavy in the air between us that neither of us wanted to be there. And that look was still lurking in Dad's eyes. I wanted to make it go away, but I couldn't say I hadn't seen the thing in the woods when I did.

"The game wasn't so bad yesterday," Dad said. "I'm sorry I fussed about it."

Dad had never apologized for an after-the-game lecture before, and there had been many of them. I shrugged a little and said, "I imagine you were right."

The word "imagine" hung in the air between us for a long minute. Then Dad sort of shook himself and stood a little straighter as he said, "I was talking to Tommy Jordan out at school the other day. He says the cross-country team can always use another runner."

Cross-country. That was something I hadn't tried. "I think I want to lay off the sports for a while," I dared to say. When I saw the look on Dad's face, I rushed on to ease the shock of my refusal. "You know, at least for the summer."

Relief bloomed on his face. "They don't run any meets till late August. You'll be good at it. I mean, you can run."

He made it sound like any fool can run, and I suppose that's true. Of course, I could also trip over my shoelaces or catch my foot in a gopher hole and come in dead last to bring the team's average down. But there wouldn't be any practices for a while, and I liked running in the woods. I could tell Dad I was training. As for the meets, anything could happen between now and then. "I don't know much about cross-country running."

Dad already took my acceptance of his new plan for granted. I'd always learned any sport he wanted me to. "I don't either, Shane," he said. "But we'll learn together." He came over and sat on the edge of my bed. I tried to remember the last time he'd been in my room to talk, but I couldn't. Usually he just hollered from the bottom of the stairs or the doorway. "Playing sports is a good, clean occupation for your body, son. I mean, when you're concentrating your whole body on obtaining a certain physical goal it keeps your mind busy, too. Sports keep you in shape not only physically but mentally as well."

When I didn't say anything—because I wasn't sure what to say—he went on. "I mean, I don't really push you to take part in sports so that I can relive my old victories. I know that's what you think sometimes, but it's not true. I want you to have your own victories."

He gave me a little shove that knocked me off my elbow and back down in the bed. "Now sleep in, sport. It's Saturday. Josephine said she wouldn't look for you until lunchtime."

"Sure, okay," I said as I curled up in my little hole under the covers again.

I waited until I heard Dad's car go up the lane before I climbed out of bed. I pushed up my window that looked out over the woods and leaned out into the morning air. Maybe was sleeping in a freshly dug dirt hole right below the window, and when he heard me, he jumped up and cocked his head at me. He didn't seem to remember his scare of the day before.

"Sure, Maybe," I said. "We'll go just as soon as I grab us both a bite to eat."

I smoothed the covers on my bed and splashed a little water on my face. I was at the top of the stairs before I thought of Tami. I went back to the bathroom and carefully soaped and rinsed my face. I didn't want to sprout a crop of zits before Monday morning. I even combed my hair, pushing the curling strands back away from my face. They wouldn't stay in place, but it didn't really matter. I wouldn't be seeing Tami in the woods. I wasn't sure what I would be seeing in the woods, but whatever it was, it wouldn't care if my hair was neat or not.

Chapter Three

I wasn't afraid when I went into the woods. Maybe I should have been. If you think about it, the woods can be a spooky place, especially early in the morning or late in the afternoon when the shadows are deep and heavy with secret beings. Or creatures, as Mr. Smithers would say. The fact that I was tracking one of these unknown creatures this morning should have been reason enough for goose bumps to rise along my spine the same way. Maybe's hair was arching up a bit on his back. He hadn't forgotten after all.

But instead the woods comforted me the way it always did when I walked into its depths. It was overgrown, wild and forsaken, everything Aunt Jo said it was when she warned me not to go into it too far. But it was also alive and beautiful. So beautiful that I sometimes stopped and clicked a mental camera so that I could preserve the sight of it forever in my head.

Now the sun was just beginning to shine through the dense branches. Up ahead I spotted a raccoon slinking out of sight, on his way home after a night of foraging.

Maybe pricked up his ears at the sight of the raccoon. Still, he stayed close in front of me until we crossed the raccoon's trail of scent. Then he couldn't resist the urge to put his nose to the ground, and with each push into the bushes where the raccoon had melted from sight, he seemed to shake off more of his timidity until he was off, canvassing the woods in front of me as he chased after first one scent and then another.

Spots of sun speckled the ground around me but there was hardly ever a patch of sun big enough for me to stand in to feel the full strength of its warmth. I was glad I had worn my old gray sweat shirt. The leaves underfoot were damp with the morning and made little noise as I moved on through the woods.

I didn't forget my purpose as I retraced my path of the day before when I had run into the woods to find Maybe. It wasn't easy. The trees and vines seemed to have changed shape overnight. I made several false starts before I found the log I had tripped over.

I wasn't very far into the woods at that point—nowhere near what I called the heart of the woods, which was my favorite spot to sit in and let the trees talk to me.

I stepped carefully over the log and then stood still and listened. Since I had no idea which direction to take from here, I began to walk in a circle to see what I could find.

I knew, when I was on the far arc of my second circle and Maybe suddenly joined me on the path, with his ears half up and half down, that I must be getting close. Actually, it wasn't really a path, only a trail of least resistance beaten down by the inhabitants of the woods. These trails wove through the trees, sometimes disappearing completely and then popping up again more noticeable than before, as if the animals had hopped out of a tree to continue their walk.

We came out into an open space under the trees. There was no sunshine: the big maple that had pushed back its competitors to make the clearing had too many leaves. Under the tree, several huge rocks pushed their tips up through a thick layer of leaves.

Maybe moved ahead of me on stiff legs as I had often seen him do when he met up with a strange dog. Perhaps that was all it had been yesterday. Just another dog who didn't take well to Maybe's friendly advances. It might even have been one of the wild dogs that are supposed to roam the woods, but I doubted it. In all my times in the woods, I'd never seen a wild dog.

Maybe sniffed the ground and then froze a moment before raising his nose to the air. He looked back at me as I stood watching him. He must have taken courage from seeing me, because he lifted his leg and left his territory markings on every tree and bush and rock he could find.

Then he trotted toward me with a look of relief that that was over with. I laughed at him and ruffled his ears. "Not so hard to take over the territory today, eh?"

He whined at me in disapproval as I moved under the tree. When I ignored him, he barked sharply, and I gave a start as though I expected something to jump down on me from the tree. I looked up, but there was nothing there. Not even a squirrel or a bird that I could see. The place was silent, almost too silent, as if everything around had hushed and was watching to see what would happen next. I could almost feel eyes on my back from the trees beyond, and a few of those goose bumps I had disdained earlier popped up along my spine.

The maple was majestic, with a trunk my arms could only reach halfway around. It had the kind of umbrella shape you usually only see on trees that grow alone and uncrowded in the middle of a field or a yard. I looked down at the ground. On the far side of the tree, big piles of leaves had been churned up in some kind of a scuffle. In one place bare ground had been exposed.

I carefully raked the leaves to one side and found a deep indention in the ground. It wasn't exactly a track, because there was no outline of a foot. It looked more like the hole a rock might make if it was pitched like a shot put. I knew about that. Dad had had me try shot-putting once.

Everywhere I pushed aside the leaves there were more of the strange holes in the soft earth. It was as if the area had been bombarded with large round rocks, but none of the rocks were still there.

I walked slowly around the outer edge of the tree where the woods pushed in on it. It didn't take me long to find the path of broken branches and trampled weeds that led off deeper into the woods. At least three feet over my head, a few branches dangled half broken but with their leaves not yet wilted. I couldn't have stretched up and broken them off.

I was trying to keep from admitting even to myself what kind of creature I thought I might be tracking. But, a small flicker of excitement was fluttering larger and larger inside my chest. I wished I'd listened more closely to Mr. Smithers' hints about the strange creatures in the woods.

Maybe put his nose to the ground in front of me once and then lagged behind. He wouldn't desert me, but he would just as soon have taken another trail. We hadn't gone far when the broken branches and beaten-down bushes stopped. One minute the trail was clearly marked, and the next there was no sign of it at all. It was as if the panic in the creature had subsided, and it had begun moving carefully once more. If only the ground were softer, I thought as I studied for footprints.

I zigzagged across the area in front of me as though I were searching for gold nuggets. By noontime I had nothing to show for my efforts except lots of briar scratches on my hands and face.

I stood up and marked the place in my mind. I wouldn't give up. I'd come back to search another day, but now I had to make tracks for Aunt Jo's.

When I called Maybe, his ears came up off his head and his tail flapped happily as we started through the trees in as close to a run as the terrain would allow. I'm lucky enough to have a good sense of direction, or I'd have been lost in the woods years ago. We headed due south, which brought us out on the road about half a mile from Aunt Jo's house. Once out on the road I settled down to a steady lope.

I liked running. I really did. I only hoped running cross-country wouldn't spoil it for me by making it into some hated exercise that had to be done correctly.

But I wouldn't think about that now. Now I'd think about the creature in the woods. I'd ruled out dogs and bears. Maybe an elephant, I thought with a smile. That would explain the deep holes in the ground and the broken branches. I laughed out loud at the idea of an elephant in Chance Woods. That would be a strange creature, all right. Then my smile disappeared as I admitted to myself that actually an elephant wouldn't be any stranger than the creature I suspected.

Even though I hadn't found the tracks to prove it, I was sure it had to be a Big Foot. There—I'd let the words come out of hiding in my mind. The excitement took wings and rose inside me. If I found a Big Foot creature, that would be better than a dozen home runs. I mean, millions of kids had hit home runs, but how many had tracked down a Big Foot?

Of course, I wouldn't tell anybody right away. Not until I had proof. And Dad would need more proof than most. I wouldn't be able to get him to go into the woods to look at a footprint if I ever found one. He'd have some kind of explanation for it. But somehow I'd prove to him I wasn't seeing things.

Aunt Jo was on the porch pretending to sweep, but I knew she was watching for me. She lives on the other side of the woods in about as isolated a place as we do, but then not far down the road new houses start popping up, and there's a regular little community called Chanceyville, with a grocery store and gas station. It's more a wide place in the road than an actual town, but some of the road maps give it a little dot. Aunt Jo and her husband Charlie used to run the store before he got sick. Then they sold out, and Aunt Jo took care of Charlie until he died two years later.

She's not actually my aunt; she's Dad's cousin once removed. I don't know what that makes her to me except a lifesaver. She took me under her wing when we moved here, even though Charlie was bedridden then and she had her hands more than full.

"What're you two running from?" she said now as she stood on the porch with her hands on her hips. She's a tiny little thing, but her frail looks are misleading. Even though she probably wouldn't weigh a hundred pounds soaking wet, she has more energy than half the kids at school. She's always into some project or another, and usually she finds a way to enlist my help. Today we were digging up a flower bed.

"I'm just trying to get into shape," I said after I caught my breath. "Dad wants me to go out for cross-country running."

Aunt Jo raised her eyebrows. Her eyes were worn and faded blue but still sharp. "Baseball season must be over."

I nodded. "Last night was the last game." The thought that I wouldn't have to stay after school for any more baseball practices made me feel like breaking out in song.

"Did you win?"

"Yep."

"Good." That's all Aunt Jo ever wanted to know. Not whether I played or hit or caught or anything. Just if we won or lost, and she really didn't care about that except that she thought maybe I did. She led the way into the house. "I was about ready to give your lunch to the cats. I didn't think you were coming."

"I always come when I say I'm coming, don't I, Aunt Jo?"

Aunt Jo's two cats, Dilly and Dally, jumped down from the couch to come meet me. Dilly was as white as Dally was black. They looked warily behind me for Maybe, but I'd made him stay outside.

"Here, kitties, leave him alone. He's got to go wash up." She gave me the once-over. "You look like you've been chasing rabbits through bramble bushes."

Aunt Jo never comes right out and asks me anything about what I've been doing, but if she wants to know, she has her ways of finding out. Most of the time I just volunteer the information right off to save us both a lot of trouble. "I was on the trail of something, but it wasn't rabbits."

She stopped in the middle of the room and stared back at me. "Has that Jake Smithers been filling your head with his nonsensical stories about monsters in the woods? Jake wouldn't know the truth if it hit him between the eyes."

"I saw something out there, and Maybe did, too." And I told her about Maybe in the woods and then about the dark shadow with the red, glittering eyes that I'd seen in the woods the night before.

"Probably a coon up a tree. Heaven knows, Shane, that the moon can play tricks on your eyes at night." She tried to put a matter-of-fact look on her face, but I saw, deep in her eyes, the same worry that had been alive in Dad's eyes that morning. Why wouldn't they just believe me? My hunt for Big Foot was harmless enough. Harmless as long as I didn't find him, at any rate.

"There's something strange out there, and I'm going to find it," I said.

Aunt Jo shook her head. "Shane, you're going on sixteen. It's time you were chasing girls instead of varmits in the woods. Isn't there some pretty little girl you're interested in?"

I couldn't quite keep my face from heating up, and Aunt Jo laughed while a little of the worry faded from her eyes. "There's hope for you yet, Shane Buckley. Now go wash up while I dip up the chili. Then you can tell me all about her."

Aunt Jo insisted I tell her all about Tami as we ate, even though there wasn't much to tell. I mean, what it boiled down to was that I thought Tami was cute, but so did just about every other male at Brookfield High. Tami thought Willie Jackson was cute, and he was a sports hero, the kind of high-school athlete the local folks would remember years from now. Me, I was a clown without even trying to be one. It didn't take a mental genius to figure out how that particular romantic triangle was going to work out.

But Aunt Jo had to know all about Tami, pulling words out of me whenever I stopped. Finally she nodded briskly and said, "She'll like you if you like yourself. You don't have to hit home runs to get a girl's attention."

"It doesn't hurt," I said as I pushed back from the table. "Shouldn't we get to digging?"

"So you don't want to talk about her with your old auntie." Aunt Jo laughed and grabbed her old army-green fishing hat from a peg on the wall and shoved it down on her head. Sharp little tufts of gray hair stuck out under the brim. Aunt Jo's hair is always sticking up wrong in one spot or another even when she fixes it up to go to church. Not that Aunt Jo cares much. Flowers and especially roses are Aunt Jo's passion.

Now, as I began turning over the moist dirt with a spade, she said, "When the roses start blooming, you can take your new friend a bouquet." The only thing Aunt Jo enjoys more than growing her flowers is giving them away. "She does like roses, doesn't she?" Aunt Jo asked and looked up at me.

"I don't know what she likes."

"Except, of course, Willie," Aunt Jo said with a wicked smile. "And I'm sure she'll love roses. By then baseball and home runs will be old news and there'll be new heroes. Maybe in what did you say? Cross-country running?"

"Yeah, sure." Even if there were heroes I wouldn't be one of them.

I was halfway through the bed, my sweater long ago discarded on the grass and my digging muscles beginning to feel a little weak, before I got up the nerve to ask, "You knew my mom, didn't you, Aunt Jo?"

There was just the slightest hesitation before she answered. "I met her a few times. I didn't really know her very well. Why?"

"Am I like her?"

"Your eyes are. She had the most beautiful eyes. So stunning that they sort of overshadowed the rest of her face, but when you really looked she had nice features, too. You remember her, don't you?"

"I remember. She was beautiful. But I didn't mean that. Last night Dad said I was like her, but he didn't mean I looked like her. He said she was always seeing things that weren't there."

This time there was a definite pause as Aunt Jo considered her answer carefully. "Your mother was a special person," Aunt Jo said at last. "I think sometimes she was meant to be a poet and just never realized it. She so enjoyed improving on the world."

"I liked her stories. They were fun."

Aunt Jo sat back on her heels and smiled at me. There was something very sad about her smile, and the worry was back in her eyes. "You are like her, Shane, in many ways. You're sensitive. You see things other people miss. But you're like your father as well. You're tough and practical when you need to be, and you're not afraid to attempt any task, however impossible it seems. Jim was never one to call quits, and I don't think you are either."

"But why doesn't he want me to be like my mother?"

"That's something you'll just have to ask Jim. I can't answer you." She bent her head back over the roses she was fertilizing.

For a long time then the only sound was the thud of my shovel as I pushed it into the earth and turned over the dirt. It was a relief to both Aunt Jo and me when Maybe decided to chase Dally up a tree. After we rescued the cat, we could talk again about cats and dogs and flowers and sunshine. The uneasiness between us disappeared like smoke in the wind, but the questions were still in my mind. Why couldn't I be like my mother? What was there about her that brought the look of worry to Dad's and Aunt Jo's eyes? And why did she have to die?

The questions stayed with me all the way home late that afternoon. I wanted to go through the woods, but the evening shadows had already begun to fall before I left Aunt Jo's. As well as I knew the woods, I had been confused about my directions often enough in the middle of the day. I thought it the better part of wisdom to stay on the road at night.

Maybe and I were almost home, running easily in the cool evening air, when the weirdest cry I'd ever heard came from deep in the woods and stopped me in my tracks. It was something between the yowl of a wildcat and the howl of a wolf, but not like either. In fact, it sounded so nearly human that the hairs on the back of my neck stiffened. I gulped in my panting breaths so I could hear better.

Maybe came over and sat on top of my feet. I touched his head; whether to reassure him or myself, I'm not sure. Night was creeping out of the trees now to surround us on the road. I've never been afraid of the dark, not even after my mother died. Then the darkness was a friend that hid my tears and sometimes brought her back to me in my dreams.

I wasn't exactly afraid of the dark now or even of what the dark was hiding, but as I heard the cry again, closer this time, it just seemed smart to put off meeting the creature who made that kind of noise until daylight. We started toward home again.

I heard Dad's car coming before I saw his lights swing around the curve. He pulled up beside Maybe and me. "You're a little late, aren't you?"

I let Maybe crawl into the back seat and then got in beside Dad. "I should have let Aunt Jo bring me home, but I thought we had time to make it before dark. You know, good running practice." I felt a little bad adding that last, since it wasn't the exact truth. Actually, I get a little nervous when I have to ride with Aunt Jo. She can barely see over the wheel, and sometimes she misses seeing little things like fences and mailboxes.

Dad laughed, pleased at the mention of running and understanding about Aunt Jo's driving. "You were probably safer on foot, all right," he said. He hesitated for a minute before he went on. "I was afraid maybe you'd cut back through the woods."

"I would have if it hadn't been so late. It's a lot shorter that way."

"Maybe you should stay out of the woods for a while," Dad said.

The words stayed in the air between us. We'd been through all this before. And I didn't like going against

Dad, but I had to go into the woods no matter what. I had thought Dad realized that, since he hadn't tried to forbid them to me for a long time. Now I kept quiet and hoped he wouldn't make his suggestion into a command.

When we got to the house, I wanted to stop in the yard and listen for the scream again and ask Dad what he thought it was, but I thought better of it. He was already worried enough about my seeing things. If I admitted hearing weird things as well, he might try to force me to give up my time with the trees. He might go so far as to have us move, as he had threatened to once years ago. I couldn't imagine life somewhere else, without the trees and the paths and the animals and Aunt Jo. Life with only school and sports.

"You're too much of a loner, Shane," Dad said now as he followed me inside. "You need to make more friends, go to the movies and such."

"I have friends at school," I said, somehow stung by his words. I might not be voted most popular, but I wasn't exactly an outcast. It was just that most of the kids liked different things than I did. They talked sports, which I got enough of at home. They talked girls, which I would have loved to join in, but I was afraid of saying something dumb and showing my ignorance. They even talked about Chance Woods, but it was a different woods than I knew. To them it was an unknown wilderness. To me it was an old friend.

My answer didn't satisfy Dad. He didn't want me just to assure him I had friends. He wanted me to have visible friends who came home with me and banged in and out of the house. He wanted me to go to the park

in town and be part of the dirt-court pickup basketball games. He wanted me to be like him.

There'd been lots of times when I wanted the same
thing, but no matter how much I tried, I couldn't be
like him. I might have liked being more popular. But
I liked being by myself, too. I didn't aim to be different from most of the other kids. I just was.

Dad sighed and said, "I just want you to be happy
and to know what you want."

"I do know, Dad. I'm going to be a naturalist." I
mean it was years away, with more studying and
school, but I was eventually going to work with nature. I knew that the way some people knew they
wanted to be doctors or teachers or football coaches.

Dad smiled and shrugged, giving in. "Today
Chance Woods. Tomorrow the jungles of Zimbabwe
or wherever," he said.

After supper, I went to my room and hunted
through my old books. I'd been heavy into strange
phenomena while I was still in grade school, and now
I reread every bit of information I could find on Big
Foot. Some of the stuff in the books was pretty wild.
There were stories of UFOs dropping Big Foot creatures off from space and that they then drew energy
from frightening people. A few Big Foot trackers believed the creatures could appear and disappear at will.
But the basic facts were all the same. A Big Foot was
a huge, hairy creature who walked upright like a man.
Its eyes were whitish gray and glowed red in the light.
It had a horrible smell and a terrifying scream. Maybe
the oddest thing of all was that there was no record of

any of the creatures willfully harming anyone, even when people were shooting at them.

I turned off my light and leaned on my windowsill. The tree frogs were in full chorus now that the nights were warmer, and here and there in the woods a whippoorwill called. I imagined all the nocturnal animals coming out of their sleeping places and padding along the paths in their nightly work of finding food. And somewhere in the depths of the dark woods there was a strange creature, his kind seen only by a few people. The legendary Big Foot. He was there. I was sure of it, and I wanted to see him for myself so badly that it hurt. And I would see him. I had to.

Chapter Four

The next day, after we ate Sunday dinner with Aunt Jo, I decided cross-country running was going to be the perfect sport for me. All I had to do was say I was going out to run, and Dad beamed. He didn't have to show me how or watch my every move to see if I was doing it right like he did when I threw a baseball or shot a basketball. He'd told me once that either you could run or you couldn't. Of course, later he might get into whether I was breathing correctly to conserve my strength for the long races or if I was swinging my arms to maximize my body's effort, but now he was content to just let me run. For even a couple of weeks of that kind of freedom, I could bear the humiliation of coming in last for a few races.

I sat down on the porch steps to put on my running shoes. Dad had bought them the day before in the city. Dilly and Dally rubbed around my legs until I had to stop and rub first the white cat and then the black one from ears to tail. Their fur crackled under my hand.

Dad and Aunt Jo's voices drifted out through the open window. I really wasn't listening until I caught my name.

"I think I've finally found a sport Shane likes and that he'll do well in," Dad said.

"Ha," Aunt Jo snorted. "He just wanted to get out to the woods." It was hard to pull the wool over Aunt Jo's sharp old eyes. I cringed a little, afraid she'd catch me eavesdropping.

"Well, he can run anywhere."

"All he's going to run into in Chance Woods is trouble. I wish you'd make him stay out of there."

"I've tried, Josephine," Dad said with a sigh. "You know I've tried, but I might as well tell him not to breathe."

"He's bullheaded like you," Aunt Jo said shortly. There was a pause, and I pushed the cats away and finished tying my shoes. I was just about to stand up when Aunt Jo said, "He asked about Linda yesterday."

"Asked what?" Dad's voice was tense.

"If he was like her."

"He's not," Dad said flatly. If he had used that tone of voice with me I would have been afraid to say another word, but not Aunt Jo.

"Yes he is, Jim. You can't take him in your hands and mold him like a piece of clay the way you want him to be, letting this bit of her personality stay and throwing away that bit. He was molded years ago, with some of you and some of Linda.''

''No,'' Dad said again, his voice even more forbidding than before.

''He can be like Linda without it meaning that the same thing will happen to him.''

One of the cats pushed his head up against my hand, and I jumped. Inside the house it was quiet, a strained quiet that seemed to crackle in the air. I wanted to stand up and yell through the window and make them keep talking.

There was a growly murmur too low for me to hear. Then Aunt Jo's voice came out as clear and as sure of the words as ever. ''You should tell him, Jim. He's old enough now.''

''No,'' Dad said. ''Not yet.''

Dilly, tired of my jerky stroking of her back, ran her paw across the bottom of the storm door. Before Aunt Jo could come to let him in, I slipped around the side of the house, behind the garage, and then ran across the narrow clearing into the first edges of the woods. I didn't want her to see me. I didn't want anyone to see me.

I kept running, dodging around the bigger trees. Learning balance, I thought grimly. That's what I'd always lacked. Balance. Dad had told me so enough times. You have to set your feet before you throw. You have to know where you are before you can learn to catch. You have to be balanced on the floor when the basketball comes your way. How do you think you'll ever get away from the tacklers if you can't keep your balance? Short kids usually have great balance, he'd said dozens of times, looking at me as if I defied explanation.

Balance was what sports were supposed to give me. Not just physical balance on my feet, but mental balance in my life as well. But sports and Dad's obsession with them always seemed to keep me tilted crazily to one side or the other. There was no balance. I was unbalanced.

For some reason that thought made me cold all over, and I fought my way through the trees as if each tree was personally trying to block my avenue of escape. I paid no attention to directions or paths but just crashed farther into the woods as though darkness were pursuing me.

When finally my breath was gone and I had to slow down, the strange panic inside me began to fade and then was gone. I looked around as though I expected that someone had witnessed my embarrassing headlong rush through the woods, but there was nothing but trees, the steady, never-changing trees. I leaned up against one of them and waited until I could quit gasping for breath.

The cold, dark worry that Aunt Jo's and Dad's words had awakened in me was still there. I knew now I couldn't run away from it, whatever it was, but I didn't understand it well enough to try to face it off. Would the questions never have answers?

I missed Maybe as I began moving along through the trees again. But we never took him to Aunt Jo's with us on Sunday. Sometimes he'd come to meet me in the woods if I could find an excuse to walk home, but today I'd gotten far off our usual path.

I began looking for some familiar tree or landmark, but there was nothing I could remember seeing before. My head was still spinning from my panic, and I wasn't even sure which was north. I wondered idly if I might be lost. The thought didn't bother me.

Later I could worry about getting home. Now it was good just to walk and forget everything but the trees. I began to name them: maple, oak, ash, sycamore. Yellow poplar, thorn and tree of heaven.

I topped a little rise, and the ground fell sharply away on the other side into a deep sink. It wasn't a sinkhole exactly, more like a large, round bowl-shaped depression, as if the underpinnings of the ground there had just grown weary and given way. Wild cherry trees stretched long trunks toward the sun, and grapevines laced their fingers around elms and walnuts. One gigantic poplar had fallen and was slowly turning back into earth. Down at the bottom of the sink, water sparkled in a small pool where a spring bubbled up out of the ground.

Nowhere was there any sign that humans had ever set foot on this spot, and I stopped at the top of the sink, reluctant to spoil the place with my own footprints.

A ledge of moss-covered rocks braced one side of the sink, and I walked softly around the lip of the crater and sat down. It was quiet there, only as it can be deep in the woods.

With a sudden flapping of its wings, a red-tailed hawk rose out of a tree in front of me. The bird had been so still that I hadn't even known it was there. I wondered how many other animals were hidden, wary of the smell or sight of me and only waiting until I had gone so that they could continue their lives.

But it wasn't me who had startled the hawk into flight after all. I hadn't heard him, but when I looked down at the spring again, there was my creature, stretched out on the ground drinking from the little pool. I caught my breath as my heart began to hammer in my chest.

He got slowly to his feet, and he was every bit of eight feet tall. His huge frame was covered from head to foot with red hair tipped in silver. The hair around his head was slightly longer, lapping down on his monstrous shoulders. He raised his arms and stretched as a man would after a nap.

No wonder Maybe had been so frightened the day he'd met this creature! I was beginning to feel more than a little quivery inside myself even before the creature froze in midstretch and started to turn toward me.

Without realizing what I was doing, I had stood up from my ledge of rocks. I hadn't made any noise, but the creature had detected my presence. We stood, both of us rooted to our spots, staring at each other.

We stared at each other for what seemed like an hour but really must have been only minutes before the Big Foot turned and crashed away through the trees. I waited until I couldn't hear the pounding of his feet on the ground before I dared to move. Even then I had the feeling that he was still nearby, still watching to see what I would do next.

Running might have been the smart thing to do, but now that the creature was out of sight, my fear began to die down. I climbed down to the spring. The stink of the creature was still there, and I covered my nose with my hand. I was sure I'd be able to find a footprint around the pool of water, but the ground was hard and rocky right up to the edge of the spring.

I knelt down and cupped my hand under the stream of water as it bubbled fresh out of the earth. The hair stood up on the back of my neck, and I had to look over my shoulder twice to make sure the creature wasn't standing right behind me, ready to rid his home territory of this pest the same way I might step on a spider that crawled into my room. I had never felt so small.

But as I climbed out of the sink, my fear changed to excitement. I had seen Big Foot. The creature existed. He had stood in front of me as real as the trees and the rocks. I wanted to run home as fast as I could and share the wonder of it with Dad.

He won't believe you, a little voice whispered in my head. You have no proof.

And there was none. No tracks, nothing except my seeing him, which should have been enough but wasn't.

I had the feeling as I reached the top of the sink that eyes were following me hungrily, not to devour me, but because the creature was as curious about me as I was about him.

I studied the area carefully, noting each oddly shaped tree or fallen branch as I moved northwest and toward home. It was late. I'd been in the woods a long time and shadows were lengthening. Darkness would overtake me soon, and then the creature's eyes following me might not seem so harmless.

After a half hour of brisk walking I came into more familiar trees, and suddenly Maybe crashed out of the bushes to meet me. I had backed against a tree at the sound of movement in the trees, sure that the Big Foot had decided to attack me after all. But it was only Maybe, wriggling all over with delight at finding me in the woods.

"You scared me, old boy. But guess what I just saw!" I said and ruffled his ears. "Your 'big turtle' is some kind of creature."

Maybe cocked his head at me and whined almost as if he understood my words.

"We'll go after him tomorrow. Only this time we'll go armed," I said. "I'll take my camera."

I was sure a picture would be enough proof for Dad. But until I had the proof I wouldn't say anything to him about the creature, no matter how much I wanted to.

Chapter Five

Not telling about Big Foot wasn't as hard as I'd thought it would be. At first I felt like bursting out with the news like I would have if I'd seen a tornado ripping through the woods or a wreck on the highway, but with them I would have had proof. With Big Foot I had nothing but the knowledge that I had seen the creature. It hadn't been a dream or the result of any overactive imagination. But I knew Dad wouldn't believe me; worse, he'd get that worried frown between his eyes.

So I kept the secret deep inside me, letting the excitement of my discovery bubble up only when I was alone in my room. Then I wrote down everything I could remember about the creature and even drew a rough sketch of it. I shoved the notebook under some old games in the corner of my closet. I loaded my camera with fresh film and got it ready.

The next day at school the time dragged by slowly. I could not thnk of anything else but going back into the woods to find Big Foot again.

"You're really in another world today, aren't you?"

I looked up from my barbecue sandwich to see that Jackie Adams had sat down across the table. I grinned, a little embarrassed. "Yeah, I guess so."

She grinned, too, and then when I looked around, she sighed and said, "Tami eats at a different time."

"What makes you think I was looking for Tami?" I asked, feeling myself blush and hoping it wasn't too obvious to the girl sitting across from me.

She flipped her dark hair away from her face. "Everybody always looks for Tami when I'm around. Nobody sees me."

I started to say something, but she stopped me.

"That's okay," she said. "I'm not jealous!" I mean, I'm not exactly ugly even if I can't stack up against Tami." She giggled a little. "I guess that was a bad choice of words, but you know what I mean."

"Sure. But if you feel like that, why do you hang around with Tami all the time?"

"I like her," Jackie said. She rearranged her food on her tray and unfolded her napkin. "Barbecue—yuck. I don't know why I even eat."

"Maybe because you're hungry."

She took a bite of her sandwich. "I'm always hungry. I'm sort of glad Tami and I don't have lunch at the same time. It makes her mad because I can eat all the time and never gain an ounce. She has a bit of a weight problem." Jackie looked at me as though daring me to disagree with her.

I didn't, though I had certainly never noticed that Tami had any such problem.

"You're stuck on her, aren't you?" Jackie asked, still holding her sandwich up in the air ready for the next bite. When I didn't answer, she laughed. It was a nice laugh. Not a titter or a giggle, but a real laugh that still didn't make me feel like she was laughing at me.

"You don't have to answer," she said. "All the boys have a crush on Tami sooner or later. It gets sort of funny after a while."

"That's me. Always the clown."

She put her sandwich down. Her smile was gone, and there was real concern in her voice as she said, "I didn't mean it to sound like that, Shane. I mean, boys just get silly about Tami." She stopped talking and looked at her plate. "I guess I'm just making it worse."

"Don't worry about it, Jackie," I said. "You didn't say anything that wasn't true."

"Would you like to meet her? I mean, really get to know her? She might like you if she knew you." Jackie looked up from her plate, and the smile was back in her eyes.

"I don't think clowns are Tami's type," I said. I wasn't sure I was ready to face the prospect of actually having to talk to Tami. I needed more time to prepare for that kind of meeting.

"You're not a clown, Shane. You're just kind of, well, different from most of the other guys who play ball and stuff."

"Different. You can say that again. Especially about sports. I hate playing ball. I always have."

Jackie looked surprised. I was a little surprised myself. I'd never admitted that to anyone before.

"Then why go out for the teams?" she said. "You're always trying out for everything. I heard you even went out for football last fall."

"Thank goodness, the coach cut me after just a few practices."

"I don't understand."

"It's a long, boring story."

"I'll bet it's not that boring."

When I didn't answer she let it drop. I liked that. Some girls can be too pushy.

"But about Tami," she said. "She's not unapproachable, if that's what you think. Of course, right now she's obsessed with Willie, but that's a passing fancy. Willie's too busy to give Tami the attention she wants."

"The season's over now," I said.

"The season's never over with Willie. He eats, sleeps and walks baseball."

"He's got big plans for the future."

"And so do I," Jackie said. "I'm going to get you and Tami together. Maybe you're just what she needs. A nice, quiet boy who has stars in his eyes for her and only her, instead of a baseball."

"You make me sound silly."

She shook her head in protest. "I didn't mean to. I mean you seem like a really nice guy. I wouldn't mind knowing you a little better myself," she said, "but I can see you haven't got eyes for anyone but Tami. And who knows? You two might make a great couple."

Neither one of us believed that, but I wasn't going to say it wasn't possible. I mean, I might not be the cutest guy in school, but I had some good points. Maybe if I got the chance to really talk to Tami, we might at least get to be friends, if not exactly a couple.

The bell rang, and Jackie groaned. "Time for class, and I haven't even eaten." She crammed a big bite of her sandwich in her mouth, picked up her tray and rushed toward the window to turn it in. I followed her.

"Don't worry," she told me as we left the lunchroom. "I'll work out something."

The rest of the day, every time I passed Tami and Jackie in the hall, my heart shot up in my throat.

Finally I decided she'd just been kidding me, having her own private joke, until in the late afternoon, while Tami was running along beside Willie and talking up at him, Jackie sent me a look and winked. Something about that wink gave me enough courage to say hi to both Tami and Willie.

Tami looked surprised but spoke to me, actually remembering my name again. Willie was even friendlier. "Hey, Shane, old buddy," he said. "What you going to do with yourself now that the season's over?"

I wondered what they all would say if I told them the truth, that I had been tracking a Big Foot. Would they be impressed? Would that be as good as hitting three home runs in a single game or throwing a nohitter? Willie had done both. But he hadn't seen a Big Foot. And I had. The thought gave me courage, and I smiled mostly at Tami as I said, "Not much."

"You know, kid, we could use a first-base coach on the softball team. Why don't you come on out when we start practice in a couple of days?" Willie turned to Tami and Jackie. "I've never seen a kid who knows more about what the other team is going to do next. I think he knows before they do." He turned back to me as though he was giving me the chance of a lifetime. "Who knows, kid? There might even be a few times when you'd get to play. What do you say?"

"That's a great idea, Willie," I said. He was trying to do me a good turn. Everybody was always trying to do me a good turn. Did I look so pathetic that I inspired pity? First Coach Wyatt and then Jackie and now Willie. I didn't want pity. I wanted to be liked because I was Shane Buckley. Still, Willie was trying to be nice. So I worded my refusal carefully. "I'm sort of taking a vacation from ball playing for a while."

"You don't want to play ball?" There was disbelief in Willie's voice, and again I found myself thinking that he and Dad were made for each other. I wondered what Willie's dad was like.

"I'm going to train for cross-country this summer," I said.

"Running, eh?" Willie said, losing interest in the whole idea. "Well, maybe you'll be good at it."

"I doubt it," I said, trying to make a little joke, and was rewarded with a giggle from Tami and a frown from Jackie. "But Dad wants me to give it a try."

"I know your dad," Tami said.

"You do?" I looked at Tami.

"Well, my father knew him years ago, and of course I've seen him at the games. My father said he was a star in high school. I think he said it was football, and that he coached before he came here." She tossed her head and giggled a little. "Of course, you must take after your mother."

I don't think she really meant for it to sound quite as bad as it came out. I mean, everybody there knew I wasn't a star athlete, but there was still an awkward little pause when nobody knew what to say next.

"I guess so," I said. "A football hero I'm not. Well, look, I've got to catch my bus. See you guys around."

I took off up the hall in a slow lope. I was, strangely enough, glad to leave them behind. Talking with Tami wasn't altogether pleasant. I mean, as much as I wanted to be around her, I was always afraid I'd make a fool of myself.

I was deep in the woods with Maybe fanning out in front of me before I let myself think about it again. Then it seemed that all I could remember was that Jackie hadn't said a single word all the time we'd talked.

The trees around me gave me confidence. I knew this world. I could spend hours here without worrying about what I would say the next time I saw Tami, or about being shorter than all the boys and half the girls at school, or about making Dad proud of me by actually smacking a ball the way a real hitter could, or about winning a race. Here it didn't matter about balls and strikes, hits or misses, wins or losses. Here the world just kept spinning and when one tree fell to time or the elements there was always another ready to take its place. I didn't want it ever to change. I wanted Chance Woods to stay wild and free forever.

Chapter Six

The creature hid from me all that week. It was there. I sensed it watching me, and twice I caught its scent on the breeze.

I tried everything. I came in through the woods from different directions. I stayed downwind of the spring. I sat without moving on the ledge of rocks until it was almost night. I kept Maybe on his leash all the time we were in the woods. Nothing worked. The creature would not let me see him. Once or twice I even wondered if it had only been a dream. But then I would feel the strange feeling that I wasn't alone in the woods, and remember the creature standing up from the spring and staring straight at me.

I still hadn't told anyone, a decision that was proving to be wiser all the time. At first I'd thought it would be as simple as leading anybody I wanted to share the secret with into the woods and letting them see for themselves. But now I couldn't even locate the Big Foot myself.

On Friday I decided to give up the search, at least for one afternoon. I tromped into the woods along my usual path with Maybe unleashed and free to run in any direction he wanted to. I paid no attention to which way the wind was blowing, and I was chomping really loudly on one of the apples I'd brought along.

I stayed away from the spring and instead headed for my special place, a place I used to think of as being in the middle of the woods, though I now knew this wasn't the case. In the days that we had first moved here, everything about the woods had been a new discovery. Of course, in those days, I'd only played about the edges. But even so, I'd felt like a frontiersman breaking trail, surveying a land for the very first time.

My mother had always been the one who shared my interest in nature. She had been the one who explored the small woods beside our house with me. Thinking back on it now, I suppose those trees couldn't really be called a woods. They were just there, spreading out in the field across the way from our house, digging their roots deep but not deep enough to stand long against the bulldozers as the town pushed out around us. I could remember when I came home from school and saw the first trees falling victim to the march of progress.

Mother had been staring out the window at the bulldozers with a funny look in her eyes. "The waste of it," she had said. "Poor trees. Not even allowed to be cut for firewood or lumber, but just shoved aside in a trash heap of dirt and bushes." And she had had tears in her eyes as she added, "Think how they must feel."

I had cried, too. Not because the trees were disappearing, though I knew I would miss our walks through the little woods, but because before I came into the house I had stood in the yard enjoying watching the big yellow dozer push the trees down. I had even imagined that I was driving the dozer myself.

I shook the memory away as I kept on walking through Chance Woods. That memory still made me uncomfortable, as if I'd somehow let my mother down. I thought how she would have loved Chance Woods. She would have understood about Big Foot. She would have helped me track him down the way we used to track down squirrels and frogs. She'd say, "Now pretend that you are a frog, Shane. Where would you hide if monstrous creatures like us were invading your territory?"

I reached my special spot in the woods still thinking about my mother. This was a place that held many memories of my mother even though she had never seen it. It was here that I'd run to during those first few months to be alone with my sorrow, and it was here that I'd finally been able to face the truth that I'd never see her again, that all my wishes and dreams couldn't bring her back.

Now I paused between two oaks that stood less than two feet apart. I looked out in front of me at a small clearing through which a stream cut. Though the stream never had much water except after a rainstorm, over the years it had dug out a deep bed, so that in some places it was as deep as I was tall. The stream was running today, pushing over rocks and digging its way a fraction of an inch deeper into the earth. I could hear the sound of rushing water even before I reached the clearing.

Maybe galloped in front of me out of the surrounding trees and headed for the creek. It was a favorite place of his as well; not only could he satisfy his thirst, he could belly flop down in the cool water.

I shucked my shoes and waded into the ankle-deep water beside him. The cold took my breath away as the water rippled across my feet, numbing my skin. After a few minutes, I climbed back on the bank and settled under a maple tree. I settled back on a cushion of last fall's leaves and stared up at the sky, far above and almost invisible through the leaves that were still on the trees.

It hadn't been a bad week even though I hadn't been able to ferret out the creature or get proof of his existence. Perhaps I should try my mother's way and pretend that I was the creature. "What would you do if someone came hunting you every day?" she would have asked.

I smiled. I couldn't be very frightening to the creature, not frightening the way I imagined that I must be to a snake or a chipmunk. They could only hide and be very quiet to outsmart me. Big Foot had more going for him than that. He was bigger, faster, and knew the woods better than I did.

Maybe came out of the stream, shook off the excess water on me, and plopped down against my leg. In an instant, he was asleep, snuffing, puffing and making little yelping sounds. A brown thrasher lit on a branch over my head and began to sing. I let all thoughts of Big Foot slip away for a minute. I'd have all of tomorrow and the next day to get back to tracking. I was considering canvassing the woods away from the spring to search for tracks. But all that would be tomorrow. Today I could just lie here and let the peace of the place wash over me the way the ripples of the creek had washed over my feet just a few minutes ago.

Jackie came into my mind, just like that. It was Jackie who had made the difference in my week at school. She had sat with me every day at lunch, advising me in between bites how I might get Tami to like me. The more she talked about it the less chance I thought I had and the more uncomfortable I felt. It hadn't been so bad admiring Tami from afar and knowing that she would never notice me. It was more restful that way. I didn't have to do anything. Now Jackie was pushing me to do more than speak to Tami.

"If you could just do something spectacular to get her attention," Jackie had said just today at lunch as she squirted catsup on her hamburger.

"You mean, like hit a home run or two?"

"No, not really. It doesn't have to be sports. You could write an article for the school newspaper. I'm on the staff. I could get it in the paper for you."

"You really think that would impress Tami?" I had been skeptical.

"Well, it might be a beginning," Jackie said. "I'm not so sure you're really serious about all this."

"Sure I am," I said quickly. "And I'd like to try writing a piece for the paper. I was thinking about getting on the staff next year anyway, but I doubt if Tami would notice my by-line or be impressed by it if she did."

"I would," Jackie said.

"Maybe so, but you and Tami aren't all that much alike."

"We're more alike than you probably think."

"You're both girls," I said. Her eyes flashed fire, and I thought for a minute she was going to throw her milk at me. So I hastened to add, "Not bad-looking girls, either."

The flash of anger disappeared in her eyes. "At least you lie like a gentleman."

"I never lie," I said. I meant it. They were both pretty girls. Maybe Jackie wasn't as eye-catching as Tami, but she was pretty in her own way. It was sort of like comparing the trees in summer and in the fall. Both were beautiful, but in a different way.

"Sure," Jackie said. "But back to cases. It's Tami you want to impress, and if you don't like my ideas, you'll just have to come up with some of your own."

I guess I was thinking about Big Foot, because I couldn't keep my face from changing expression.

"You *have* got an idea," Jackie said. "I can see it in your face. Here I have been racking my brain, and you've been plotting on your own. Let me in on the secret."

"It's not exactly secret, but I'm not ready to tell anybody yet."

Jackie gave me a considering look like the one I'd gotten the first day we sat together at lunch. "Tami won't be that impressed with a cross-country track win," Jackie finally said, but hesitantly, as though she didn't want to deflate my hopes.

"I know, and I don't expect to be a winner anyway. Still, it might not be so bad being on the cross-country team. I sort of like to run, which is more than I can say for any of the other sports I've tried."

"I'm thinking about going out for the team myself," Jackie said and looked down at her plate again while a flush crept up in her cheeks. It was the first time she'd shown any hint of shyness.

"You're kidding," I said. She certainly looked the part more than I did, but cross-country wasn't a very popular sport at our school.

"No, I'm not kidding. Do you think you're the only kid who ever wanted to be a sports hero?"

"I don't want to be a sports hero."

"Why not just quit, then? Do something else. Get on the annual staff. Write for the newspaper. You have a good voice. Maybe you could sing with the chorus. Why knock yourself out playing ball if you don't like it?"

The bell had rung then, before she could ask any more questions. We'd separated in the hall to run to our classes. I'd been in such a hurry that I'd forgotten to watch for Tami in the crowd of kids that pushed against me going the other way.

Now I lay half asleep under the trees and tried to come up with an idea for a news story. Jackie had said I'd have to have it ready by Monday and that I could write about anything I thought would be interesting to the kids at school.

Maybe noticed the smell before I did. He raised his head and whined before scrunching closer against my leg. I came sharply back to my surroundings. The light had dimmed in the woods. I'd been there longer than I'd intended to stay. Then the smell came rolling over the creek, almost overpowering me, and every nerve in my body tingled awake, because I knew the creature was—had to be—very close.

As Maybe began to growl deep in his throat, I grabbed his collar. The books were all clear on one thing about Big Foot creatures. They didn't like dogs, and I wasn't taking any chance that Maybe would suddenly leap away from me and run after the Big Foot.

The creature looked the same way I had sketched him after my first sight of him, except he appeared even bigger this close to me. He was squatting there on the other side of the creek in the same position a man would squat down next to a fire. I had the feeling that he could be up and gone in a second, but he didn't move so much as a muscle even after I sat up and returned his stare.

His face showed no expression, although he had his head cocked to one side as if considering what sort of puny little creature I was. His reddish silver-tipped hair hung down over his forehead, falling into his gray, nearly colorless eyes. His mouth was slightly open, and I could see teeth but no fangs. One arm stretched down to the ground. The other arm was propped on his knee, and the hand dangling in the air looked big enough to palm a wrecking ball.

I wished I had the camera I had left at home, even though the light was really too dim for picture taking. Still, he was so close. In fact, he was so close that I hardly dared breathe for fear of scaring him away.

We stared at each other for a long time before I worked up the nerve to try to make friends. "Hello," I said. My voice came out high and squeaky, as though it hadn't been used for a year.

The creature jerked his head back a little at the sound and seemed ready to jump to his feet and take flight if necessary. All my muscles were tense and ready as well, but I thought it wouldn't do me much good to try to run from the creature. If he wanted to catch me, he only had to take one stride to my three. Yet the longer we sat staring at each other the less afraid of him I became. He'd had the chance to hurt me while I was half asleep but he hadn't. He could even have hidden and watched me without showing himself, the way I knew he'd been doing all week.

I remembered the other apple I had in my pocket. I pulled it out and held it toward the creature. This time he did spring to his feet, unfolding from his squatting position with athletic ease and perfect balance. Standing, he towered over me. Maybe's growl rumbled out of his throat into a bark, but the sound was hesitant and he didn't pull against my hold on his collar. I kept holding the apple out in front of me, although my hand wasn't as steady as it had been.

"It's just an apple," I said calmly, as though he could understand me. "You can have it."

But the creature had seen enough. He opened his mouth wide and made a low groaning sound. Then he turned and walked away into the trees. I watched him. I never took my eyes off his back even for a second, but he just disappeared into the trees. I could hear him, but I couldn't see him anymore.

I waited a long time before I let go of Maybe. Still, the crazy dog bounded across the creek and paid no attention at all to my commands that he come back. I ran after him, but he didn't go past the spot where the creature had sat. I waited while Maybe sniffed and pawed at the place and then wet it down with his own scent. As soon as he had established his dominance of the place, we crossed back over the creek. I placed the apple in the very middle of the spot where I had been lying.

Dad was already eating when I got to the house. Neither of us likes to cook, and so we eat a lot of soup and sandwiches. But tonight Dad had brought home chicken with all the fixings, and I knew he was upset that I hadn't been at home when he got there, although he didn't come right out and say so.

I jabbered out my excuse. "I'm sorry, Dad. I sat down and almost went to sleep. It got late before I realized it."

Dad looked up at me and shook his head. "Sometimes I wish we'd moved to the middle of a city somewhere." He sighed. "Go wash up. The chicken's already getting cold, and you smell as if you've been in a hog pen. What did you get into that smells like that?''

I just shrugged and ran upstairs. I hadn't realized that the odor of the creature had clung to me, but now I caught a whiff. It wasn't the greatest smell, but at least it was some kind of proof that I hadn't imagined the whole thing, that it hadn't been a dream.

When I came back down the stairs I could see Dad sitting at the table. He was nursing a cup of coffee and reading the paper, and though he was turned to the comics, there was a frown etched between his eyes and he looked bone-weary. I'd hardly ever seen him look so tired. He usually shook off the worries of his day as easily as shucking his jacket and tie. He always had the energy to pass a few balls or take me to a game. Even before Mama died and while he was still involved in his coaching, there had always been time for playing ball with me. And then it hadn't been the chore it became after I was old enough to compete. It had been fun to chase down the balls I missed while Dad coached me on what I had done wrong and Mama put in an encouraging word.

He heard me on the step then and looked up and smiled. I knew I was the cause of his worry and, worse, that I had been for years without ever being able to do anything about it.

Dad put down the paper while I ate the chicken that was no longer warm. I even ate the cold gravy spread out on the biscuits. It wasn't bad.

"Were you out running?" Dad asked.

I nodded. "If they ever have a meet where I have to dodge trees, I should win hands down." I was sorry as soon as I mentioned the woods, because the frown inched back into Dad's eyes. "Of course, the cross-country team doesn't start until school starts."

"Tommy Jordan said that he'd have a couple of meetings this summer just to organize the team and that he likes his team members to run in some of the local road races. Just to sort of get in shape."

"Sure. Why not?" I said. "But I don't know if I can run well enough to win races." I thought it would be better if Dad didn't build up any unrealistic hopes about my running ability.

"Maybe you'd rather play softball this summer?" There was a hopeful look in Dad's eyes. He really wasn't that keen on any sport that didn't require the use of some sort of ball.

"I don't think so," I said. I hated to disappoint Dad, but it was either now or on the field this summer. "Why don't you join one of the men's teams?"

"I might, if it wasn't for my knee." He punched at his knee as if he were still angry at it for failing him while he was in college. After an operation, he'd finally had to drop out of the football team in his senior year.

"You could coach a Little League team. They're always begging for coaches in the paper, and you used to do a great job with our team when I played." Sometimes I thought that if I could just get him back into coaching, he would be happy the way he'd been before we moved here. Before Mama died.

"Yeah, some of the kids went on to make pretty good ballplayers."

He didn't look at me, and I was glad. We both knew I wasn't one of his success stories. There were times, and this was one of them, when I wished I could just blink my eyes and become the son Dad wanted me to be. I'd be a few inches taller, lean and mean, with muscles in all the right places and balance, great balance. I could keep my curly hair and blue eyes—it couldn't possibly hurt for me to be that much like my mother. The image of a super-me faded in my mind. Actually, except for wishing I was a little taller, at least an inch or so taller than most of the girls, I wasn't that upset with the way I looked. And it was only to please Dad that I ever worried about my lack of balance on the athletic field.

The silence stretched between us while the only sound was the crunch of the chicken I ate. I wondered if the Big Foot had come back to the creek and eaten the apple, or if maybe a raccoon or possum had found it. It would have made a small mouthful for the Big Foot.

"Somebody called you a while ago," Dad said.

"Oh, yeah? Who?" I asked. I didn't get many calls when I wasn't on some kind of ball team.

"I don't know, but it was a girl," Dad said, with a smile playing around his eyes. "Maybe you can tell me who."

My face fired up. I couldn't help it, and Dad laughed.

"It was probably just Jackie Adams. She wants me to write a story for the school newspaper. She's on the staff."

"What are you going to write about?"

"I was thinking about a piece on all the old legends about Chance Woods." I sort of held my breath while I waited for his reaction. "What do you think?"

He answered carefully as he got up to refill his coffee cup. "That might be interesting, although most of those stories have little basis in fact."

"That wouldn't matter if I was writing about legends. Mr. Smithers is always telling me about this person and that person who disappeared into the woods and were never seen again. Of course, that was all years ago, and I've never been able to believe that people could get lost in the woods."

"Not everybody has your woods sense, Shane. It would be easy to lose your way in there."

"Sure, to lose your way, but not to be lost forever," I said. I pushed on determinedly. "And then there are the stories about strange, lurking creatures. Sometimes I wonder if Mr. Smithers hasn't seen something strange in the woods himself. He acts like the trees spook him sometimes. He's always warning me about the creatures in the woods."

"He's just an old man who likes to tell tales, and with you he's found a good listener." Dad's voice was tight. "Too good, I'm afraid."

"But if he really saw something weird like that, shouldn't he tell somebody?"

"Nobody would believe him. Everybody would just think he was a crazy old man. It could be the school board would even make him quit driving his bus, and then what would he do?" Dad's words carried a warning.

"I wasn't going to mention any names or state anything as fact. Just legends, or what you might call believe-it-or-not stories. That couldn't hurt, could it?"

"I don't know, Shane. I don't suppose so, but it might be better if you just interview Coach Wyatt, now that baseball season is over. Or Willie. I hear he's going to go down to the Brave's tryout day."

"Yeah, so I heard." I put my chicken bones back in the box and stuffed it in the trash. "But somebody is always writing stories like that. I want to do something different—'The Legends of Chance Woods.'" I shrugged and added, "The editor of the paper may not like it, anyway."

Dad didn't even try to hide the worry as he looked at me. I wanted to tell him about seeing the Big Foot more than I'd ever wanted to tell anybody anything, but the words stayed deep in my mind, away from my tongue.

Dad looked down and studied his cup of coffee. He was alone again, even though I was in the same room with him. With a sharp stab of pain, I remembered my mother again and the time she was sick. Most of that time was a haze to me, a haze I deliberately made so the pain wouldn't be so intense. It had been a bad time. I didn't remember much else besides that, but now I remembered my dad coming in after a game or practice and sitting at the table drinking coffee all alone while the house just sort of seemed to close in around us.

I couldn't stand it. I said, "Don't worry, Dad. I'm not going to do anything too dumb."

I didn't think he heard me. I'd never been able to say or do anything to take the worry out of his eyes. I was at the stairs when Dad spoke.

"Shane, some things shouldn't be told. Ever."

Chapter Seven

I went through the woods early the next day on my way to Aunt Jo's. My camera hung from its strap around my neck. As I walked I practised raising it to my eye and focusing it quickly in the shadow of the trees. I was going to be ready this time if the creature should suddenly appear in front of me.

The apple was gone, but I couldn't be sure the Big Foot had taken it, even if Maybe did stalk stiff-legged around the spot while the skin on his head wrinkled with concentration. Then he jumped down into the creek bed and barked sharply before he grabbed something. It was only a poor turtle that immediately retreated into its house and locked all its doors.

"You silly old dog," I said with a laugh. "You'll just get tired of carrying him and drop him about a half mile from here. It'll take the poor thing a week to get back home."

Maybe wagged his tail and then lay down with the turtle between his paws to wait for me to be ready to leave.

I was about to climb back out of the creek when I noticed a heel mark in the soft mud around the pool of water. Even the partial print was larger than my own foot. I searched around the creek then, but I could only find what might have been the impression of several toes. I snapped a picture of the first heel print, but even as I did it, I thought it would take a lot of imagination for anyone who hadn't seen the creature to believe it was a footprint. Dad didn't have that much imagination. That was for sure.

I found the widest and muddiest spot in the creek and put an apple on each bank. Now all the creature had to do was oblige me by stepping in the mud. In spite of his wariness, I couldn't believe he purposely avoided leaving tracks.

All at one I felt a little wary myself. I stood up slowly and really searched the shadows around the clearing, but I couldn't see anything out of the ordinary. Still, I knew he was there even if I couldn't spot him or even smell him. He was there.

As I moved away from the creek toward Aunt Jo's house, Maybe picked up his turtle and trotted behind me, panting in bursts around his mouthful of shell. When he didn't seem to be aware of the creature in the shadows, I decided that probably I was just wishing the Big Foot was there. I tried to stop looking for the creature behind every tree and instead just enjoy the morning.

Chance Woods was particularly pretty that morning. There had been a light shower during the night, but now the sun was shining. The sunshine glinted off every drop of water it could reach through the tree leaves. There was a damp, growing smell in the air, and the violets and wood anemones almost seemed to burst into bloom as I passed by them. I took several pictures. I tried to get a shot of a squirrel as it peeked around the trunk of a tree at me, but it ducked away just as I clicked the shutter. The Big Foot, if he was there, stayed out of my sight.

I didn't get back again to the woods that day. I think Aunt Jo and Dad had a conspiracy to keep me too busy to go into the woods. No matter how hard or fast I worked, there was always another chore waiting. Dad wouldn't even fall for the excuse that I was going to run. We cleaned house, mowed the yard, repaired the fence and even cut some wood, although it would be months before we would use the fireplace again.

However, Saturday wasn't a total loss. Aunt Jo talked about some of the legends about the woods after I told her I was writing a news story for the school paper.

"Of course, I don't believe half of any of this," she warned me after a particulary farfetched story of a boy who had been seen riding a wolf. "Though I never was really sure about the baby that was supposed to have been found in there. I don't think the animals fed it or anything, but you never know. Somebody might have left a baby in there. I mean, you read in the papers about people throwing them in trash cans and all sorts of horrible stories that to me don't sound a bit harder to believe than someone leaving their baby in the woods."

"If that was about fifteen years ago, I might believe the baby was me," I said, thinking that might explain a lot of things.

Aunt Jo, who has never been slow on her feet, frowned at me. "Now you just hush that nonsense. You're every bit a Buckley."

"I've never been able to prove it to Dad."

"He doesn't want you to prove anything to him, Shane," Aunt Jo said gently. "He just wants what's best for you. It hasn't been easy for him since your mother died, but he's tried so hard to be a mother and a father to you. As hard as you could ever expect anybody to try. Right now you're his whole life."

"I don't want to be his whole life, Aunt Jo. I can't live out his dreams for me. I just can't. I'm me. A little shrimp of a fellow who knows trees and directions but who can't catch a touchdown pass or even hit a baseball so that it goes past the second baseman if my life depended on it."

"None of that matters."

"To Dad it does."

"Not as much as you think," Aunt Jo said. She put her weather-roughened hand against my cheek. "There are just some things you can't understand until you're older."

"I am older," I insisted. "I could understand if anybody would give me a chance. Or at least I could try."

She sighed and dropped her hand back down to her side. "I know," she said. "I know that and you know that. But your father isn't sure yet. He's worried about you and this woods thing."

"But I've always spent a lot of time in the woods."

"Too much. I used to be sure you'd get lost in there and we'd have to call out the National Guard, and even with their tracking dogs or whatever we'd never see you again." She tried to make a joke of it, but I knew there was more than a little truth in what she said.

"You don't still worry about that, do you?"

"No. I've decided that you're half fox or deer. Or maybe skunk." She wanted to laugh and change the subject. Most of the time I would have let her, but I kept remembering how Dad had looked in the kitchen the night before.

"What is it about me that scares Dad? You'd think I had some kind of incurable disease."

A strange look flickered across Aunt Jo's face before she put both her arms around me, something she hadn't done since I got to be taller than she is. "He loves you, Shane. It's as simple as that. He loves you, and people worry about the ones they love."

I didn't have the heart to say any more about it. I hugged her back and said, "You're the only person in the world who can make me feel tall."

And then we laughed and went back to working with the roses.

That night I tried to put on paper the stories I'd been told about the woods. It wasn't as easy as I had thought it would be. I had to be careful not to mention any names and at the same time make it all seem as if there just might be a bit of truth in the stories. That was easier to do when I began writing about the creature, because I knew the truth about Big Foot.

"Besides swallowing up hapless members of the human race, Chance Woods has in its time been a sanctuary for a variety of strange creatures," I wrote. "There have been sightings of a large, prehistoric bird and of snakes that would rival the circus sideshow boa constrictors. There have been reports of everything from killer bees to overgrown lizards, not to mention Big Foot creatures. In fact, it seems that few people want to mention Big Foot, but the story of such a place as Chance Woods would not be complete without a Big Foot, the legendary half-ape, half-man creature. He's generally seven or eight feet tall, six or seven hundred pounds, and with a generous covering of hair. Our own particular Big Foot is said to have reddish hair tipped with silver and, of course, the obligatory enormous feet that leave the only proof of its existence in most places.

"Legend, fantasy or fact? One thing is sure: there's more to Chance Woods than trees."

It was late when I finished spilling the words out on the paper. I read them over and frowned. It wasn't great, but then maybe, just maybe, it wasn't totally bad either.

I shoved it aside and went to bed. I lay awake a long time listening to the sounds of the woods coming through the open window. There was no noise from the Big Foot that night, but he was out there somewhere among the trees. Remembering my story, I thought words were just too inadequate to really describe a creature like him. Words couldn't convey the power of the creature's body or the mystery of his existence. A Big Foot couldn't exist, and yet I had seen one. And I would see him again, and this time I'd have my camera. A picture was worth a thousand words. Especially to my father.

The next day I didn't get to go into the woods either in spite of all my plans. After Sunday dinner with Aunt Jo we came home to find a bright blue bike leaning against the yard fence.

"Looks like we have company," Dad said.

All the way home I had been studying the edge of the woods, planning a new attack and wondering how much time I would have before the light faded. "Company?" I said. I didn't keep the disappointment out of my voice.

Dad laughed. "Maybe you won't mind this company so much. It looks like a girl's bike."

Jackie was sitting on the front steps stroking Maybe's head. Maybe had his nose on her knee soaking in every bit of her attention, so much so that he hardly looked our way when we drove up and only reluctantly tore himself away to come greet us at the gate.

Jackie stood up awkwardly, as if she wasn't quite sure of her reception. "Hi, Shane," she said. "I hope I haven't come at a bad time."

"Of course not," Dad said. He was beaming first at her and then at me. "Well, Shane, aren't you going to introduce us?" he asked finally.

"Yeah, sure, Dad. Jackie, this is my Dad. Dad, this is Jackie Adams. And you've already met Maybe."

"Maybe?" she said.

"The dog," Dad said with a laugh at her puzzled expression. "It's a long story. You'll have to get Shane to tell you about it sometime."

"Sure," I said again, but I didn't offer to explain Maybe's name. Not right then.

Dad gave me a little frown. Not the worried frown I had come to dread, but the aggravated frown that I earned when my performance at sports didn't exactly please him. He smiled at Jackie again. "Do you live close by?"

"Well, actually, it's several miles, but it was such a pretty day and I like to ride my bike. It keeps me in shape."

"I wouldn't have thought your parents would have let you come by yourself. That stretch of road through the woods is sort of lonesome."

"Well, actually I'm pretty independent," Jackie said, though her smile faded a little. "They don't worry about me too much."

I rushed to her rescue. "The woods aren't so bad in the daytime. It's only after dark that some people think they get sort of spooky."

"I can understand that," Jackie said.

"When you get ready to leave, Shane will ride out to the other side of the woods with you. Okay, Shane?"

"Sure, Dad." There was no arguing with Dad when he used that tone of voice. Even Jackie recognized that. She gave Dad a wary look, but she didn't protest.

"Shane knows the woods like the back of his hand," Dad said. The note of pride in his voice surprised me. "He can name all the trees for you as you pass them."

"That should be interesting," Jackie said in a polite you-have-to-humor-adults tone.

I tried not to smile, and I guess even Dad realized that he'd come on a little too strong, because he said, "It's nice meeting you, Jackie, but I've got some work to do. So I'll just leave you two kids alone."

After he had gone in, I said, "Don't pay any attention to Dad. He worries too much sometimes."

Jackie smiled. "I thought it was sort of gallant of him to be worried about my safety. And to give you the chance to be my protector. Do you really know the names of all the trees?"

"Sure," I said. "All but one. I've worn out at least three tree books trying to figure out the name of it. I think maybe the only one is in Chance Woods."

"And nobody has ever seen it but you?"

"Maybe not," I said.

"I'd like to see it," Jackie said.

I hesitated. The woods had always been mine and mine alone. I wasn't sure I wanted to share even so much as a scrubby little tree, but I managed to make myself say, "Sure, sometime when you're dressed for it." I looked down at her long, slender legs and jerked my eyes quickly back to her face. "I mean, the briars and weeds would eat you up."

She was smiling as if something had either amused her or pleased her. I wasn't sure which, but I was afraid it was the first and she was laughing at me. But she only said, "Okay then, it's a date. I'll wear my hiking boots in case of snakes. I've never really been in the woods. They say it's easy to get lost."

"You won't get lost as long as you're with me."

Again the smile came back to her face, and this time I was sure she was pleased. She changed the subject. "I really didn't mean to just show up on your doorstep like this, but I tried to call and I couldn't ever catch you at home."

"Then why did you think I'd be home now?"

"Actually, you weren't. I've been waiting. I mean, everybody comes home sooner or later, don't they?"

"Usually," I admitted.

"I thought I'd come over and help you with your news story. It has to be ready to print early in the morning, and I wasn't sure you knew how to set it up. I can take it home and type it for you if you want me to."

"I wrote it last night, but I don't know if it's any good."

"You say that about everything you do. Sometimes I wonder about you, Shane Buckley."

"A lot of other people do, too," I said.

She punched my shoulder and laughed. "Let's see your story. It could be you're right and that it stinks."

"Well, what do you think?" I asked, after I'd given her time to read it.

"I don't know," she said and looked back down at the papers in her hand. "It's different from anything we usually print, but it's interesting."

"Thanks," I said.

"A little strange also. I mean, I've heard a few stories about the woods, but nothing quite like this. Who told you all this?"

"A good reporter never reveals his sources."

"Have you seen any of this stuff? Are there really giant snakes in there?"

I laughed. "I've seen some snakes, but none are that big."

"I don't like snakes," she said.

"That bothers you more than the thought that you might meet up with a Big Foot?" I asked casually.

"There's no such thing as a Big Foot," she said. "But there are snakes."

"How do you know there's no such thing as a Big Foot?" I asked. "People have sighted them in other places."

"People *say* they've seen them. That doesn't mean it's true. People say all sorts of things to get attention."

I didn't say any more. What could I say? I'd been on the verge of telling her about my Big Foot, but now the words sank back deep in my mind. I looked down quickly as she turned to me. I didn't want her to see my disappointment. I said, "Maybe I should take that part out."

"No," she said. "No. It adds to the piece. After all, it is about legends and rumors and such, not fact."

"I could just write something else. Something that has more to do with school."

"You don't have time," Jackie said and began folding up the papers until she made a small enough square to fit in her pocket. "I'll take it and type it up for you. Tami should be impressed."

"Tami?"

"Yeah, remember? That's why you wrote this. So that you could impress Tami. You hadn't forgotten that, had you?"

"Of course not," I said. I'd been so wrapped up in tracking the Big Foot that I hadn't thought about Tami all weekend. "But I still don't think she'll be too impressed with this," I added.

"She'll be impressed. I'll see to it." She had the grace to grin after that last remark.

She had a nice grin that set her eyes to dancing, and I smiled back.

"Well, if you're going to escort me through the dark and dangerous forest, Sir Lancelot, the time has come." She stood up. "My mother might worry if I don't get home before dark. I wouldn't bet on it, but she might."

I went around to the shed in back of the house to get my old bike. I hadn't ridden it for at least a year, and I had outgrown it the year before that. But if the tires would hold air I could ride it standing up.

Dad had already pulled the bike out of the shed and pumped up the tires for me. He'd even wiped the dust off the rusty red fenders. I had the feeling that if he could have, he would have produced a brand new ten-speed bike like Jackie's for me.

Jackie laughed when I came around the house on the old bike. I shook my head at her and said, "No fair making fun of Sir Lancelot's charger."

"It looks more like a Shetland pony."

"Go ahead and laugh, but if you want me to go with you, this is the best I can do."

"I wasn't making fun, Shane. Not really. It's just that you look so big on that bike."

"Never apologize for thinking I look big," I said. I patted my handlebars. "This old bike might not look like much, but I used to have a lot of good times on it before..." I hesitated. I'd been about to say before Mama died. I changed it to "before we moved here."

We pedaled along in silence for a while. Jackie kept her pace slow so that I could keep up with her. Then all of a sudden, Jackie blurted out, "Is it awful not having a mother?"

I didn't answer right away. I wasn't sure what I should answer.

Jackie looked over at me and said, "I'm sorry. I shouldn't have asked that. Sometimes my curiosity gets ahead of my good sense."

"That's all right. It's just that nobody has ever asked me that before."

"Well, of course it must be awful," Jackie said, jumping in on the end of my words. "It was a dumb question."

"How would you feel if you lost your mother?" I turned the quesiton on her.

She looked straight ahead, and her forehead wrinkled with concentration as she pumped the bike pedals slowly and steadily. "I can't really imagine it. I mean, I know I'd be sad, but I just can't imagine Mama not there, never seeing her again. I don't like to think about it."

I nodded. "I miss my mother. Even now after all this time, I still miss her. You know, I see something in the woods and I want to show it to her. I'll think, Mom would have liked that. She was always so much fun. She used to make up little stories about the silliest things."

"What kind of things?"

"Oh, I don't know. Just anything. Like we'd see a grasshopper and Mama would say he was on a trip around the world trying to forget his sweetheart who had hopped away with a cricket." I smiled to myself at the memory. "But all Mama's stories were happy in the end." I was a little embarrassed at having told Jackie about the stories. They had always been a secret between my mother and me. I'd never shared them with anyone, and I wasn't sure I should have now. "I guess that sounds dumb to you," I said.

"Not really. She must have been a wonderful mother." Jackie slipped off her bike to walk beside me up a hill that was too much for my small bike. "How'd she die?" Then she added, without giving me time to answer, "If you don't want to talk about it, you don't have to."

"It's all right. I don't mind, but really I've never been sure what was wrong with her. She'd been sick, you know. It seemed like months, but I don't know if it was really that long."

I paused, but Jackie didn't say anything. After a moment I went on. "The day she died I was there with her. Dad was still at school. He was at practice. He'd told me to take care of her like he'd done since I was old enough to understand the words. He would say that we men had to take care of the woman in our lives. It was all just a joke, you know, but then after Mama got sick he kept saying it, and nobody smiled anymore because Mama did need somebody to take care of her."

I hadn't realized I'd stopped walking until Jackie stopped beside me. I looked away from her toward the trees and wished I could just leave her there and go back through the woods. She put her hand on my arm, and my muscles stiffened.

"I'm sure you did the best you could," she said gently.

I shifted away from her touch and started moving my bike up the hill again. "No, I didn't. I thought she was just asleep. She had some pills to help her sleep, and she'd get tired and tell me she was going to take a nap. That day she was asleep when I got home from school. At least I thought she was asleep. And then later I couldn't wake her up." My voice was a little shaky as I said, "I don't want to talk about it anymore, Jackie, if you don't mind."

"Okay," she said and pedaled out in front of me for a few minutes to give me a chance to get hold of myself.

I looked at the trees and made my mind a complete blank. I didn't want to embarrass myself by crying.

"You're amazing," Jackie said as we pulled out into the late-afternoon sunshine on the other side of the woods. "How can you remember the names of all those trees? I'm impressed." She slid half off her bike seat and put one foot on the pavement to balance her bike.

"There's nothing special about it. You just have to look at them and see the difference between them and then be curious enough to want to know what to call them. Then it's just like knowing a rabbit from a chipmunk."

"I can tell those two apart." Jackie laughed. "Well, thanks a lot for seeing me through the woods. I can make it the rest of the way on my own."

"You could have made it this far on your own, and a lot faster if you didn't have to wait for me. It's just that Dad has never been really comfortable with the woods so he gets overprotective."

"After reading your piece about all the strange goings-on in there, maybe we should all be nervous." She smiled at me and got up on her bike seat again. "I'll see you tomorrow at school, if one of the Chance Woods creatures doesn't come out of the trees and carry you off."

I watched her pedal out of sight before I turned my bike around and started for home. Maybe got up from his resting place in the shade and trotted beside me. "She's nice, isn't she, old boy?" I said. Maybe barked companionably at me as if he couldn't agree more.

Now that I was alone again, I was much more aware of the woods. The late-afternoon shadows spread all the way across the road, and only in a rare spot here and there did a sliver of light from the sinking sun reach through. It would be too late to go into the woods by the time I got home, and I felt a stab of disappointment. I had been so sure that this was the day would be able to capture Big Foot on film.

Still, I was glad Jackie had come. I was even glad we had talked about my mother. I wanted to remember and talk about her. With Dad and even with Aunt Jo I felt the shutters go down as soon as I mentioned Mom.

Suddenly I felt I wasn't alone on the road. I looked over my shoulder, but there were no cars coming. Not too many came along this stretch of road.

He was there, watching me from the trees. I knew that even before I smelled the rotten odor and before Maybe's fur inched up on his neck. I stopped my bike and studied the trees. Maybe hunkered against my leg and panted rapidly, even though the air was cool here in the deep shade of the trees.

"Where are you?" I said aloud. My voice sounded thin and lonely on the evening air. There was no answering movement or sound, and I began to believe that the only times I would ever see the creature again was when he allowed it. I'd caught him unawares at the spring, but he wouldn't let that happen again.

Yet he must be as curious about me as I was about him. Why else was he standing hidden in the trees and watching me?

I rode on toward home with a rising sense of hope. The creature had allowed me to see him once. He would again. And the next time I'd have my camera ready. I didn't think past getting the proof of his existence. Time enough then to worry about showing it to Dad. Or maybe Jackie.

She'd laugh. I knew she would, but that wouldn't matter. She'd be impressed too.

Chapter Eight

The school newspaper printed my article, but only after Jackie used her considerable powers of persuasion.

"It's not that they didn't think it was good, but we haven't printed anything all year that didn't have some kind of school connection, no matter how slight," Jackie explained at lunchtime. "For instance, if the janitor's son had seen one of those creatures, that would be a school connection."

I laughed. She had intended for me to laugh. I said, "They don't have to print it if they don't want to. My ego isn't that fragile."

She shook her head. "They're going to print it. It's either that or a blank half sheet of paper, because I didn't turn in the story I was supposed to be working on."

"You shouldn't have given me your space, Jackie."

"I wanted to." She shrugged. "Besides, your piece is much more interesting than mine—what the kids are planning to do this summer after school lets out. And I used to think adults had boring lives."

The bell rang, and we took our trays to the window. Then, as we were leaving the cafeteria, about to go opposite ways down the hall, Jackie said, "I told Mrs. Smith you wouldn't care if she offered your article to the *Brookfield News*." When Jackie saw the doubt on my face, she rushed on. "They might not print it, but if they do, you'll be famous and Tami will fall into your waiting arms."

Her words didn't exactly reassure me. I not only couldn't imagine Tami falling into my arms, I also couldn't imagine what I would do if she did. But that wasn't the real reason for my doubt. I asked, "What will Dad say?"

Jackie was halfway down the hall, about to be swallowed up by a rush of kids. "He'll be proud," she called back to me.

I doubted that even more than Tami falling into my arms.

I finally got back among the trees that afternoon. The apples I'd left in the creek bed were gone, but there were no monster-size footprints. There were raccoon tracks and a fox track and the signs of several deer coming to this pool to drink. Any of them might have taken the apples, but for some reason I was sure that it had been the Big Foot. I smoothed out the mud around the pool of water and placed two apples on either side of the creek again. I still couldn't believe the creature was purposely avoiding leaving his footprint.

He let me see him again that night as I was leaving the woods. I heard something behind me, and when I turned, he was there, close enough to be able to reach out with his long arms and grab me. My heart began thumping heavily as I stared up at his face.

The light was dim and the shadows were deep, but I raised my camera to my eye and snapped a picture anyway. My quick movement and then the noise of the camera shutter terrified or infuriated the creature—I wasn't sure which. Nor was I sure if he was about to lunge at me or away from me. I could only stand in terror and wait for whatever was going to happen, because no matter how I had romanticized Big Foot in my mind, he was still a wild creature. A very large wild creature who could swing his club of a hand and bounce me out of his way as easily as a bear swatted away a bee.

"I didn't mean to scare you," I said. The words came out not much above a whisper. Maybe, his loyalty overcoming his fear, jumped between the Big Foot and me and began barking, edging a bit closer to the creature and then springing back. I wanted to reach down and grab his collar, but I couldn't move.

The creature squalled and swung halfheartedly at the charging dog. The blow sent Maybe reeling. I forgot my fear as I ran to Maybe. For a minute he lay totally still, and I was afraid the worst had happened. But then he whimpered and licked at my face as I leaned over him, almost as though he was embarrassed by his failure to protect me. I buried my face in the fur of his neck. After a minute, I looked over my shoulder to see if the creature was about to finish us both off, but he was gone.

Maybe just had the wind knocked out of him. He got to his feet shakily, shook himself a little and followed me meekly the rest of the way to the house.

I stopped trembling on the outside before we left the trees, but I still felt a little tremor inside me. It was late that night before I could convince myself that the creature never intended to hurt me. It had been my fault for being overeager to get his picture, a picture that probably wouldn't even come out.

Tuesday my article came out in the school paper. A dozen kids who had never spoken to me before in all the time I'd been going to Brookfield High stopped me in the hall to tell me they'd read my story and then to ask if I'd seen the Big Foot. Each time I managed not to lie without admitting the truth.

On Wednesday the article was printed in the Brookfield weekly paper. Jackie gave me a copy of the paper at lunch. She was beaming.

"Yesterday you were famous schoolwide. Today, countywide. Tomorrow, who knows?"

"You think maybe the Associated Press will pick it up?" I tried to make a joke. Actually, seeing the article with my by-line was giving me mixed emotions. The *Brookfield News* wasn't a big paper, but it did have a healthy circulation, and the fact that they had thought my words good enough to print made me feel great. Yet at the same time, as I skimmed over the piece, I couldn't get rid of the uneasy feeling that Dad wasn't going to be proud or even pleased. Of course, it wasn't on the front page but was stuck inside out of the way. Maybe he wouldn't see it.

"You're not happy," Jackie said, her own smile fading.

"Sure I am," I said. It was only partly a lie. I didn't want Jackie to feel bad.

"I just don't understand you, Shane Buckley. You wanted Tami to notice you and I try to help you out, and what do you do? You sit there as if you wished the words would disappear right off the page."

"I don't know if you could say that," I protested.

Jackie didn't want to listen. She stood up and said, "Maybe you just want me to disappear, too. Well, that can be arranged. I'm good at arranging things."

She stalked out of the cafeteria, leaving her untouched lunch on the tray across from me. I looked down at my tuna sandwich, white cake with chocolate icing, and green jello cut into neat little cubes. Without touching a bit I stacked the two trays and took them to the window.

Tami stopped me in the hall after school to tell me she'd read my article. "Now, how much of it is the truth?" she asked with a little giggle.

I looked past her to Jackie, whose eyes shot fire at me. "I guess all legends have at least a germ of truth in them." I turned my eyes back to Tami.

Tami was saying, "I'm having a little get-together Friday night to celebrate the end of school. You can come, can't you?"

"Sure, why not? I haven't got plans."

She gave me a funny look, and I supposed I wasn't enthusiastic enough. I was beginning to decide there was no pleasing girls.

That afternoon I could hardly wait to get back among the trees. Even Maybe seemed to have forgotten his confrontation with the Big Foot and moved ahead of me with his usual spirit. I hadn't forgotten. The sense of fear and helplessness I had when I was standing in the creature's shadow, with no means of defense, burned in my mind. But the creature hadn't hurt me. He hadn't even really hit Maybe very hard. Besides, I doubted whether I'd see him that day, since I was pretty much convinced his terror had matched my own. And even if I hadn't been sure of all that, I would still have had to come into the woods. I needed its peace around me. I needed the security of the unchanging sameness of the trees. Everything else might change, but the trees were always there, solid and strong.

It was on days like this that I said a little prayer of thanks for old Mr. Chance's eccentric ways. Now, as I walked deeper into the woods, I thought of all the stories I'd heard about Mr. Chance. There were lots of them, since his life had become part of the legend of Chance Woods. They said he lived to be more than a hundred, but nobody was actually sure how old he really was. He claimed not to be sure himself. And in his later years he was as apt as not to meet you at his gate with a shotgun. He said he didn't need anything but his trees, least of all people. One story even had it that Mr. Chance was the reason people who wandered into his woods disappeared.

I didn't believe he'd ever killed anybody. I thought he was just an old man who needed the solitude of his woods just as much as I needed it now. Was that what worried Dad? Was he afraid I was going to become a recluse like old Mr. Chance? Today I felt it might be a possibility. At least here in the woods I didn't have to worry about not understanding girls.

I was thinking so hard that the footprint in the mud didn't register right away. It wasn't Big Foot's. It was a man's boot print. A sharp feeling of loss went through me. In all the times I'd come to this place, I'd never seen any sign of a human being. In other parts of the woods, yes, but never here. Never in my special place.

Two squirrels chattered to each other far above my head. A rustle in the brush caught my attention. A deer was standing in the shadows, probably waiting for me to leave so that he could get a drink. I couldn't see or hear anything that told me the man who'd left the footprint was still around, but I felt uneasy. I kept imagining him standing in the shadows just as I'd imagined Big Foot doing in the past few days. But though I hadn't minded the idea of the creature watching me, I minded the idea of this new intruder very much.

After a long time of listening and watching, I took a flat-edged rock and wiped the man's footprints until nothing but the smooth earth remained. But I couldn't wipe away my feelings.

Chapter Nine

Dad was quiet as we ate our supper. I suppose I was extra quiet myself as I thought about the intruder in my woods. Of course, I knew the woods weren't actually mine, though I would have liked to own every acre so I could take over where Mr. Chance had left off as protector of the wildness of the woods. I reminded myself that I really had no proof that the man who had crossed my creek intended to spoil any part of Chance Woods, but the thought didn't make me feel much better.

As for Dad's silence, I just figured he'd had a hard day on his sales route. I knew that though he was successful at it, he didn't enjoy the work. I didn't think I'd ever understand why he had quit coaching. Once I almost mentioned the open coaching job at Brookfield High again, but I thought better of it and stayed silent. I had all but forgotten the article in the paper that I was so worried about at noon.

"I've been thinking," Dad said as he began clearing the table.

I looked up at him warily. I could tell by his voice he had made some sort of decision, and I had the sinking feeling that this decision had something to do with me.

He had his back turned to me as he carried the dishes to the sink, so he didn't see my face. "I have a friend who runs a summer camp for kids. It's sort of a conservation camp where kids learn about our natural resources and things like that."

"I'm too old for camp," I said.

"I know that, but I think he would hire you as a counselor." He turned and looked at me. "He said his counselors were usually at least sixteen, but I told him how much you knew about trees and nature, and he thinks maybe he can bend the rules."

I looked over at the window. It was dark outside, but I could imagine the trees beyond. I said, "I was thinking I'd classify the trees in Chance Woods this summer. Maybe write them all down by species."

Dad clamped down on his irritation and kept his voice enthusiastic. "The trees will still be there when you come home, and this is a chance to see new forests and broaden your horizons a little." Dad was working up his sales pitch. "You'd get to make a little money, though the pay isn't much, and you'd make a lot of new friends. I'm sure some of the other counselors would share your interest in trees and nature."

When I didn't say anything he went on. "I've been through the area, and it's beautiful country, with rock mountains and hardwood forests and lakes. It's a great opportunity, Shane."

I tried to imagine it. I really did. Just like I'd tried all those other times to hit or throw the ball the way Dad said. But I couldn't.

"When?" I asked.

Dad sat down across the table from me. For a minute, just for a minute, I felt sorry for him before I hardened my heart.

"The second week in June through the third week in August."

"All summer?"

"You'll get to come home some on weekends, and I'll be on the road a lot this summer anyway."

He'd always been on the road a lot, and I'd always stayed with Aunt Jo. That had never been a problem before. This was worse than playing softball. "What about the cross-country team?" I asked, hoping I'd found a way out.

"You'll be back in plenty of time to try out for the team if you want to, and you can keep training at camp. You'll have free time."

"Why?" I asked. A half dozen questions circled in my brain. Was he trying to get rid of me? Had he found a woman friend? In all the time since Mama died I was sure he hadn't seen another woman, but now as I looked at him, I wondered at that. Dad was a nice-looking man. And not as old as I'd once thought.

He was so long in answering that I knew the answer. I said, "You saw the paper."

He nodded. "I saw the paper."

"Jackie said you'd be proud." Bitterness crept into my voice.

He got up and walked across the room to lean on the sink and stare out of the darkened window. "I am proud of you, Shane, but I'm worried about you, too." He spoke to his reflection in the window. "The forest has gobbled you up. You depend on it for everything. For friendship, work, sport. It's becoming an obsession with you. Sometimes I wish we'd never moved here."

"Why did we then?" I asked.

"I needed to get away from people, and Josephine was close by to help take care of you when I was on the road. It seemed the ideal place then."

"I'm glad we moved here," I said softly.

Dad turned from the sink and looked at me. "I want you to take this job, Shane."

I didn't say I would. Always before when Dad said something like that to me, I would agree because I knew it was what he wanted, and even though this was an opportunity that on another day I might find interesting, tonight I couldn't agree that I would do as he said.

After a long silence, I said, "I saw the Big Foot, Dad. I've seen him three times, once as close to me as you are now."

Dad looked as if I had kicked him in the stomach, but he managed to take hold of himself. When he spoke, it was calmly and reasonably. "Sometimes our imaginations play tricks on us."

"I saw it, Dad." I tried to keep my voice from shaking. "I've been trying to take a picture of the creature, because I knew you wouldn't believe me, but I saw it."

Dad still looked sick. He seemed to be searching his mind for something to say. Finally he just repeated what he'd already said. "Sometimes our imaginations play tricks on us."

"Does yours?" I asked. I sat without moving in my chair as though I were calm, but inside my chest my heart was pounding every bit as hard as it had the day I'd faced the Big Foot on the path.

"I used to imagine I was a better football player than I was," Dad said.

"That hardly compares to seeing a Big Foot, does it?" I didn't like the hint of sarcasm that I heard in my voice; it came out without my realizing it. A part of me wanted to run to Dad and admit I hadn't seen a thing even if that would be a lie. At least it might wipe that frown from between his eyes. But another part of me wanted to stand my ground, to make him believe me, to know he trusted me.

"You didn't see a Big Foot," he said. "There's no such thing, Shane," he said gently.

I should have kept quiet then. I didn't want to upset Dad, really I didn't, but I couldn't keep from asking, "Did Mom's imagination play tricks on her, too? Is that why I'm too much like her?"

His face went gray. "I don't want to talk about it anymore," he said. His voice was too quiet, too calm.

He turned to go into the small room off the kitchen that he used as an office when he was home. He paused at the door and said without turning around, "You are going to the camp, Shane. It's too good an opportunity to pass up."

"Why can't I be like my mother?" I asked loudly, but the door shut on my words. I wanted to follow him into his office and make him explain, but I couldn't. I never went into his office. It was his sanctuary just as mine was the woods. The trouble was, I thought as I looked out the window at the night, I couldn't escape into the trees at night.

I climbed the steps to go to bed. This had to have been the worst day of my life since my mother died. I didn't sleep well. I wrestled with the Big Foot and saw him shot by the stranger in the woods. Jackie kept storming away from me every time I tried to talk to her, and once I thought I saw Dad standing beside my bed and smoothing the covers up over me just like Mama used to do. That dream seemed very real, but when I opened my eyes there was nothing there but the dark.

The next day, Thursday, ranked right up there alongside of Wednesday as a horrible day. Jackie didn't come sit across from me at lunch. She sat all the way across the cafeteria and wouldn't even let me catch her eye. It didn't matter that two other girls sat there and talked to me about my article in the paper. They weren't Jackie.

Finally I picked up my tray of food, which I'd hardly touched, and carried it up to the window. I wasn't even smart enough to take my tray up at the same time she did hers. She was already going out through the swinging doors. Maybe it was just as well. I wouldn't have known what to say anyway.

After school I escaped into the woods. I wasn't sure what to expect. I had the spooky feeling that people were watching me from behind every tree. Not just people—intruders.

Then he was in front of me almost as if he was waiting for me. Not the Big Foot. I would have been happier if it was the creature who was blocking my way through the woods. Instead it was a short, barrel-chested little man. Of course, he was taller than me, but not by much. He wore drab brown and green clothing that blended in with the trees, and he carried a rifle slung over his shoulder. His cap was pulled low on his forehead and shaded his eyes and face. I looked down at his boots and knew that he was the man who had left the track by the creek.

"I thought it was about time for you to be getting here," he said. He stepped a few paces closer. I had to keep myself from backing away from him and trying to disappear into the trees the way Big Foot did. But I stood my ground, and now I could see the man's face better. His skin was weathered and creased, and his eyes had a determined look.

"Who are you?" I asked.

"McMurtry is my name." He wasted no time in coming directly to the point. "You're the kid who saw the Big Foot."

"Where'd you hear that?" I asked. "I never said anything about seeing a Big Foot."

The little man waved his hand; he was obviously impatient with any sort of word games that might waste his time. "You wrote the piece in the paper. My brother saw it and called me."

"Why should he? It was just a piece about the legends of the woods." This intruder was in my woods because of what I had written. The thought wasn't comforting.

"My whole family thinks I'm a little touched in the head," the man said as he backed over to a tree and leaned against it. He shifted his gun so that it wouldn't hit the tree trunk. "But they indulge me. You see, I hunt Big Foot creatures."

He saw my eyes go to his gun, and he pulled it off his shoulder and propped it on the ground. He said, "Oh, this ain't for the creatures. Guns don't do them much harm, according to most of the folks who've tried shooting them. Did you shoot at yours?" He peered at me with narrowed eyes.

I didn't answer. The man in front of me was so strange, so different from anybody I'd ever met, almost like an oversized fairy-tale dwarf instead of a man, that I was beginning to wonder if Dad was right and my imagination was playing tricks on me. First with the Big Foot and now with this strange little man.

"But of course you didn't," he said. "You ain't the shooting type." His eyes went to Maybe, who was watching him from beside my leg but with his tail wagging and his ears cocked, ready to make a new friend. "That your mutt?" the man asked.

I nodded.

"Come here, pooch," the man said and patted his leg. Maybe looked up at me and then sidled over to the stranger and let him pat his head.

"Your dog's too trusting, kid," he said. "Let's see, what is your name now? I saw it in the paper." He pulled a newspaper clipping out of his pocket and looked at it. "Oh, yeah, Buckley. Shane Buckley." He stuffed the clipping back into his pocket. "Well, you might as well tell me about seeing the Big Foot, Shane."

"I just wrote about legends," I said. I called Maybe back to my side and then kept my hand on his head while I talked. "Stories folks around here have told me, but I don't think any of them actually saw any of the stuff I wrote about."

"Nice speech, kid. Might be convincing, too, if I didn't have a sixth sense about this kind of thing. As soon as my brother called yesterday and read me the part about the Big Foot, I told myself that this kid had seen something. I've been hunting the Big Foot nigh on fifteen years. In that time you get to recognize the truth when you see or hear it. You can tell the people who have sighted one by the look in their eyes."

"Have you ever seen a Big Foot?" I asked.

"Nope, never have."

"Then why do you think they exist?"

"Because I've talked to people like you who have seen them, and I've seen their tracks. Oh, I'd like to see one, and I will someday. Maybe even this time." Even in the shadow of the trees I could see in his face how much he wanted that.

"What would you do if you saw one?" I asked.

"I'd kiss the Mother Earth it was standing on, and then I'd get help and I'd capture the thing. Then everybody would have to believe that the creatures do exist."

I looked around at the woods—my woods—and imagined it overrun with men like McMurtry, carrying nets and guns and traps. And it would all be my fault. "If a creature like that existed, you could never capture him," I said.

"It ain't never been done yet, but that don't mean it ain't possible. Especially if a body is determined." He stuck his head out a little from his body and said, "You have seen one. What'd it do? Disappear in front of your eyes? They're good at that."

"I haven't seen anything," I said. "I haven't seen a Big Foot or a giant bird or even so much as a wild dog in these woods."

He leaned his head back against the tree and gave me a considering look. "You lie better than I would have thought you could, Shane, old buddy. But why are you lying? That's the million-dollar question. And where did you see the creature? And when? I'd pay you for telling me what you know."

He didn't look as if he had enough money to pay for his own supper. I said, "I could use some extra cash, but my father taught me not to lie."

"Okay, kid, whatever you say, but I'll be around. Watching and waiting. When you're ready to tell your story, just look over your shoulder and I'll be there."

"You'll be wasting your time following me around. One thing for sure, I'm not a Big Foot," I said. I couldn't bear the idea of him stalking me in the woods.

"Yeah, but you've seen one, and from the way you act, I'd say he's taken a shine to you. They'll do that sometimes. He'll come out where you can see him again, and when he does I'll be two steps behind you."

"You're crazy," I said.

"So I've been told," he said and smiled in a mean way.

I left him there by the tree. I was relieved when he didn't try to follow me right away. I cut across the woods and began to run as soon as I was out of sight. It took me only a few minutes to get to the creek.

I looked down at the smooth patch of mud I'd made the night before, and my heart sank. There in the middle was the clearest, most perfect Big Foot track you could ever want to see. It looked so perfect in fact that I wondered if maybe the strange little man I'd just left had planted it there. But then Maybe sniffed it and backed away with his ears flat against his head.

With the same rock I'd used the night before to get rid of the man's footprint, I scraped away Big Foot's. I worked fast. I wasn't sure when the man would pop out of the woods behind me, I just knew that he would. But I had already filled the muddy space with rocks so that new footprints wouldn't show and was on the way home before I heard McMurtry coming through the woods after me.

I stood still for a minute and looked at the trees. Hide, creature, hide, I kept thinking over and over.

Chapter Ten

Friday ought to have been a great day. The fact that it was the last day of school in itself should have been enough to make it a banner day. Then there was Tami's party that night. Tami, the girl I had wanted to date all through my high school days, had actually invited me to one of her parties. I'd have the chance to show her that tall and athletic wasn't all that was important. I'd be able to let her get to know the real Shane Buckley. But I wasn't looking forward to going to Tami's house.

I hadn't even wanted to come to school. But whoever heard of missing the last day of school, unless maybe you had a raging case of measles? After all, the only reason you went the other nine hundred ninety-nine days was to get to the last one.

At lunchtime I decided Jackie must have the measles. She didn't come into the cafeteria, and I hadn't seen her in the halls all morning. In my mind I had made up a fancy little speech to recite to her. First off I was going to apologize for being ungrateful. Though at this point I felt that her idea of that story in the newspaper was the cause of most of my problems. I mean, Jackie wouldn't have disappeared from the cafeteria and school campus, Dad wouldn't be banishing me to camp, and that strange little man wouldn't be stalking my woods searching for my "imaginary" creature if I had written about the win-loss record of the Brookfield High baseball team the way Dad had wanted me to.

As I left the lunchroom and headed for my afternoon classes, Tami touched my arm as we passed in the hall and said, "Don't forget about the party tonight at seven."

I should have been excited about that at least. Even in my wildest fantasies I'd never had her touching me and singling me out in front of all the other kids. But now all I could say was, "Have you seen Jackie? She's not sick, is she?"

Tami's smile widened a little, and her eyes lit up as if she knew a special secret that she wasn't going to share with me. "She's not sick," she said as she moved on toward the cafeteria.

I was tempted to skip class and just search the halls until I found Jackie. After all, I had searched the woods, which had a lot more hiding places than the school, and I had found the Big Foot. I could find

Jackie. But I went to class instead and tried to be patient as the minutes ticked away slowly.

At long last we had our grades tucked out of sight in our pockets and we were free of school for months. I had about two weeks before I had to go to the camp, because although I hadn't yet said I'd go, I knew I would. I always did what Dad wanted me to do. And maybe it wouldn't be so bad. Not nearly as bad as the year he sent me to football camp. That week was so bad that I had blocked it out of my memory. I was pretty good at doing things like that. So good that now when I tried to remember what had been so bad about that week, I really didn't know. All that was left of that week in my head was that I knew it had been bad and that I had disappointed Dad again.

Maybe it would be good to get away from it all and go to this camp Dad had picked out. There wouldn't be any sports except maybe a pickup game of basketball or volleyball. I wouldn't mind that, and Dad had said there would be trees. By August, McMurtry would probably have given up the search. I figured if he'd been hunting all these years and hadn't sighted one of the creatures yet, my Big Foot wouldn't be the first.

At home, Dad and I pretended we hadn't disagreed the night before. I didn't mention the Big Foot and neither did he. Twice I caught his worried eyes on me, and I wanted to tell him I would go to camp, but I couldn't seem to speak the words out loud. Not yet.

"So who's this Tami?" he asked as he drove me to her house.

"Tami Collins," I said. I tried to describe her to him. "Medium height, great shape, blond. She came to most all of the baseball games."

Dad sort of nodded his head. He wouldn't remember her from the games. All he remembered from the games were the plays and the players, not the spectators. He said thoughtfully, "There were some Collinses back in Whitesburg." There was a touch of worry in his voice. "But then I suppose Collins is a pretty common name."

We hardly talked during the rest of the drive to Tami's house, which was only a few miles from ours. Dad seemed preoccupied, as he did every time the old town was mentioned, and I had my own worries. I was going over for maybe the thousandth time what I would say to Jackie. I had the words polished until I was sure they would slide off my tongue with hardly any effort at all on my part.

I'd say, "Please don't be angry." I thought "angry" sounded better than "mad." "Please don't be angry with me, Jackie. I value our few weeks of friendship, and I don't want to lose it over something as silly as a newspaper article." The whole thing was silly, so silly that I was beginning to wonder if that was really what Jackie was so upset about.

I told Dad I would hitch a ride with Willie back to Aunt Jo's house and just spend the night there so he wouldn't have to come back after me.

"Have a good time, Shane," he said and sounded as if he meant it. He was happy I was going to a party. He had as high hopes for my social life as he did for my athletic career. Poor Dad. He'd been good at everything in high school, a popular superathlete. No wonder he was disappointed with me.

Tami met me at the door. "Hey, Shane, I'm really glad you came," she said and gave me one of her brightest smiles.

"It was great of you to ask me," I said politely. I looked past her to see if I could spot Jackie, but I couldn't. Tami had a new guest to greet anyway, and she didn't miss me when I edged away from her.

The room was already crowded, even though I was a little early. I knew most of the kids. I'd been on some kind of sports team with all of the boys. A few couples were dancing in a small cleared space in the middle of the room, and others were grouped around a table of chips and snacks. Since I couldn't see Jackie, I figured that would be the safest out-of-the-way spot to wait until she got to the party.

The last party I could remember going to I had spilled some punch and then crawled under the table to hide when a little girl laughed. Mother had been there. She'd coaxed me out from under the table and laughed and made it seem totally normal for me to feel like retreating for a while. The rest of the party had been fun.

I held onto my glass of soda and backed up against a wall so I could keep my attention on the door. I couldn't believe Jackie wasn't coming. She and Tami had been friends forever, and Jackie would come. Maybe I could get up the nerve to ask her out to a movie before I was banished to the outer limits for the summer.

The talk and the music drifted around me. It wasn't a bad party. There were plenty of Cokes and chips and six kinds of brownies. I counted them.

Five minutes crept by, and then ten. After fifteen minutes, I decided I had to know for sure if she was coming or not, even if it meant making my way across the crowded floor over to Tami and coming right out and asking her where Jackie was. But I was saved from that fate; an empty chip bowl and pitcher needed refilling.

Tami, being a good hostess, noticed the empties, and when she came over to remedy the situation, I followed her toward the kitchen.

"Oh, hi, Shane. Are you having a good time?" she said.

"Yeah, sure," I said.

Tami smiled a little and then made a face. "I asked too many people again. I always do. I just can't seem to limit my number of friends, if you know what I mean."

"Yeah, sure," I said again.

"But then I guess it's kind of cozy when we all get mashed in here together," she said with a grin and leaned against me a little as we inched our way through the kids that were between us and the kitchen. "Here, you can help me with the chips," she said and handed me the bowl.

"Is Jackie here?" I blurted out.

She looked at me over her shoulder and giggled a little. "I told Jackie that you were interested in her not me, but she said I had rocks in my head. Jackie always thinks I have rocks in my head, but sometimes she's wrong and I'm right."

She hadn't told me what I wanted to know, but I was too embarrassed to ask her again. Anyway, we were pushing into the kitchen, and there was Mrs. Collins cutting up some kind of gooey brownies. She looked up at Tami and said, "Did you invite the whole school, dear? If you keep having these parties, we're just going to have to get us a bigger house." Then she saw me behind Tami. "And who is this? I believe he must be a new one."

"This is Shane Buckley, Mom," Tami said. "He's looking for Jackie."

The two of them exchanged a look and a grin. They were a lot alike except, of course, Mrs. Collins was older. Mrs. Collins was cute, blond and had a smile that kind of dazzled you. "Oh, how nice," she said.

"We came back for more food. They're eating like animals," Tami said as she tore open a sack of chips and poured them into the bowl I was still holding.

"Well, you go on and take that back out, dear. I'm sure Shane won't mind waiting until I get these brownies arranged on the plate to bring them out, will you, Shane?"

"No, of course not," I said. I could hardly say I'd rather be anywhere than there with Tami's mother trying to think of something to say to fill up the silence that Tami left behind her.

I shouldn't have worried. Mrs. Collins didn't need any help in making conversation. "Are you new around here? I don't recall seeing you at any of Tami's parties before."

"I guess we don't exactly hang out with the same bunch," I said. "But my dad and I moved here about four years ago."

"Oh, really. Where did you live before?"

"Over at Whitesburg."

"I grew up in Whitesburg, and so did Harold." She smiled over her shoulder at me. "We both still have family over there. It's a nice little town."

"Yes," I said.

"I knew some Buckleys." She stopped digging the brownies out of the pan and turned to look at me. "Of course, I see it now. You must be poor Linda Buckley's son. I went to school with her, you know."

I didn't say anything. For some reason, I didn't like the sound of her voice when she mentioned my mother, but Mrs. Collins didn't notice. She turned back to her brownies and said, "She was such a quiet, sweet little girl. It was hard for me to believe it when I heard she killed herself."

It took a minute for me to really understand what Mrs. Collins was talking about, but when I did, it hit me like a sledge hammer. I couldn't move or speak.

"Of course, I knew she had had a nervous breakdown," the woman kept on. "I wanted to go to the funeral. Linda and I had been fairly close in school. But Tami had a dance class that day and Harold was out of town. I sent flowers."

Suddenly she seemed to realize I was too quiet. She put the last of the brownies on the plate, picking up several and rearranging them as though their position on the plate was important. "I want you to know how sorry I was about it all. I know it must have been hard on you and your father," she said softly without looking directly at me.

She picked up the plate and handed it to me as though she expected me to carry it back out to the party. Instead I ran out of the kitchen, pushing past people without knowing who they were or what they were saying about me. I just knew I had to get out. I felt as though I couldn't breathe. Finally I reached the front door. I grabbed the doorknob and opened the door.

Then somebody took hold of my arm. "Shane! What's wrong? Shane!"

It was Jackie, but I had to keep running. If I stopped I would cry, maybe even scream. I mumbled something that she couldn't understand before yanking my arm away.

I raced across the lawn out onto the road. The sound of my feet pounding against the pavement gave me a feeling of power. Then I heard someone running up behind me. "Shane! Stop! Tell me what's the matter!" There was something in her voice that got through the roaring in my head. A part of me wanted to stop, but at the same time I just couldn't. I had to get away.

After a while she stopped chasing me.

Chapter Eleven

I couldn't think—I just kept running. The lights of cars slowed and then passed by me. It didn't take me long to cover the distance between Tami's house and Aunt Jo's. Aunt Jo had the light on in her front room, and even from the road, I could see her sitting in her favorite rocking chair. She'd be working a crossword puzzle with Dilly curled in her lap.

I wanted to run up the drive and burst in on her and make her tell me the truth. She knew. She'd known all the time, and she'd kept it from me just like Dad. But I didn't need to hear the truth from them. I already knew the truth. I'd always known. All it needed were Mrs. Collins's words to break down the defenses I had put up against remembering.

I ran past Aunt Jo's house, just slowing down for a second. My mother had killed herself. My mother had been *crazy*. My father and Aunt Jo were both afraid I would be like my mother. No, my father thought I was already like my mother. Hadn't I seen things? Things that couldn't be? Maybe this camp he was sending me to was really for emotionally disturbed kids.

I kept running toward the woods. The trees seemed to hold out their arms in welcome. I left the road and plunged into the underbrush. I wanted to be swallowed up by the darkness. I felt as though I never wanted to see or hear anything ever again.

I couldn't run in the woods. I wanted to run, to hear my feet slamming into the earth and taking me farther and farther away, but I kept stumbling over vines and crashing into branches. I had to slow to a walk while my eyes adjusted to the shadowy darkness of the woods.

I didn't know where I was in the woods or even in which direction I was moving. I didn't care as long as it was deeper into the forest. I wanted to hide.

But I couldn't. Oh, I was hidden from the world. No one could find me that night. The woods had closed around me, swallowing me, but it wasn't protecting me. It wasn't closing away the truth. Instead the truth had run every step with me and was there now leering out of the darkness at me.

I walked until my feet wouldn't move anymore—they just seemed to stick to the ground. I leaned back against a tree. The bark was knobby and uncomfortable, and I thought it must be a hackberry. I slid down to sit on the damp ground. I was glad the tree's bark bit into my back.

It was a long time before I could think sensibly. I wanted to concentrate on happy memories of my mother. I tried to recall them, but they kept slipping away, and all that would come were images I had buried deep in my mind long ago. I kept seeing my mother as she had been when she was sick. I saw again my father's frown as he pleaded with her. I didn't remember the words, but the frown was etched in my mind. It was the same frown he wore when he looked at me now.

All these years he had been shielding me from the truth, trying to protect me, trying to make sure that I didn't become like my mother by attempting to mold me in his own image. That's why he had pushed me into sports and hated the woods that called to me. He was afraid for me to be alone too much, afraid that a seed of insanity would somehow take root in my head just as it had taken root in my mother's.

She had lost all grasp of reality, and somehow her life had gotten intertwined with the small clump of trees that had surrounded our house. She had tried to stop their destruction. She had gone out and wrapped herself around one of the trees in front of the bulldozer.

I remembered it so clearly now that I wondered how I could have blanked it out for so long. She had been wearing her bright blue bathrobe. The wind had flapped it back away from her bare legs, and she'd looked so pale against the working tan of the bulldozer man. He had tried to make her move, but I had attacked him before he had a chance to touch her. I couldn't stand the thought of him laying his hands on her. The man wasn't being cruel. I knew that now. I could see the confusion in his face as easily as I could feel it even now.

My father had come home and unwrapped my mother from the tree. Then he had carried her inside and put her to bed, and the bulldozer man had pushed over the tree. My mother never looked out the window again, and two days later I couldn't wake her up.

Was it any wonder that my time in the woods worried Dad? Was it any wonder that he was afraid of my resemblance to my mother? Maybe it was something to be afraid of. Maybe the trees were an obsession with me that I would allow to take over my mind. Maybe I had already. Maybe I had only imagined the Big Foot.

The thoughts circled in my mind like buzzards searching for something rotten to land on. But I had seen the Big Foot! The creature was real and not my imagination, no matter how unlikely that seemed. I knew the difference between real and imaginary things. I might be like my mother in many ways, but I wasn't my mother.

In fact, when I realized that truth, I knew I had to go home. A few minutes before I couldn't stand the thought of facing my father, but now I wanted to see him. We had to talk.

I pushed up off the ground and began walking, but I couldn't tell where I was in the woods in the darkness. I hunted for clear spaces between the trees, but it was too cloudy to see. I had an odd feeling the woods was turning on me, holding me against my will, closing off all avenues of escape.

I walked slowly and hesitantly, but I kept banging into tree branches until I finally accepted the fact that I couldn't find my way out of the woods in the darkness. I found a maple tree by feeling the bark and pushed up a bed of last fall's leaves. The night air was chilly, and as I pulled some of the leaves over my legs I wished I had warmer clothes than the ones I had on for the party.

I wondered if the party was still going on, if Mrs. Collins was still baking brownies, and if the room was filling up even more. It seemed like days since I had dressed in my best clothes and rehearsed my speech to Jackie and gone to the party. I'd never gotten to say my speech, and now it didn't seem to matter. I'd never be able to explain what had happened to me tonight to anybody. Not even Jackie.

Aunt Jo might understand. I thought again of how I'd seen her head rocking back and forth in her window when I'd run past her house. All at once I wished Maybe was with me, with his head in my lap. I needed the touch of something alive and warm.

I didn't sleep well. I kept dozing off only to be jerked back awake by some noise around me. The animals of the woods were going about their business as usual. They paid no more mind to my presence than if I were a new rock dropped down from the heavens. Once I heard the Big Foot cry close by, but now that I knew the creature who made the sound, it didn't frighten me. In fact, hearing him was almost reassuring, as though it was proof that my imagination wasn't playing tricks on me.

Finally I opened my eyes to the dim light of morning. The thick gray dawn was pushing back the black of night. A possum scurried past me. He didn't give me so much as a curious glance as he hurried back to his home tree to begin his day's sleep.

I sat without moving, even though my muscles were begging to be stretched. The early-morning birds were beginning to sing. A little chipmunk ran up onto my shoe and sat there a minute before he realized his perch was a little strange. He scampered back to the ground to twitch his nose and stare at me.

But I could sit still for just so long, and as the first rays of the sun began making their way down to me, I stretched. The leaves scattered about me, the startled chipmunk disappeared into the ground and a deer that I hadn't even spotted crashed away through the trees.

I was stiff, chilled to the bone and hungry. I wanted to go home, but at the same time I dreaded it. The worried look would be in Dad's eyes, and now I would know why.

I walked for an hour before I admitted to myself that I was lost—more than bewildered; actually lost. I hadn't seen anything familiar, and I realized that I must have gone much deeper into the woods during my headlong rush the night before than I had ever been before.

I sat down on a boulder to get my bearings. I wasn't worried yet. I had confidence in my ability to find my way out of the woods eventually. I wouldn't become one of the legends told about the woods, though I thought, with a wry smile, that it might be one of the more interesting stories. Boy Who Sighted Big Foot Runs Away From Party and Disappears Forever in Woods.

But my father would never believe it. He'd know I was in the woods, and he'd search until he found me, dead or alive. Dad had to know the ending of every story, and the ending had to make sense. Probably that was why he couldn't face my mother's death. Nothing about any of the stuff remembered during my night in the woods made sense. She had been so happy, and then with no reason she became so unhappy. Dad wouldn't have been able to accept that any more than he could accept my disappearance in the woods no matter how many stories of Big Foot creatures and UFOs the local people told.

I'd never been in this part of the woods before. I would have remembered the big boulder I was sitting on and the cedar tree across from me that looked as if sheer age had split it right down through its heart and made it fall to both sides. But I knew my directions now. It had taken just a minute for me to push all my other worries aside to let my mind clear. I had to go north to get home.

Still, when I got up and began walking, I lost my concentration, and after a long time I found myself back at the boulder.

The woods seemed extra quiet around me, as though every living thing was waiting to see what I would try next. Again I had the uncomfortable thought that the woods had turned against me. I was responsible for the intruder coming into its midst, and now the woods was punishing me. The thought made me wonder if I might not be going crazy after all.

I didn't see the Big Foot come out of the trees. He was just suddenly there, watching me in his silent, steady way. Or at least I thought he was there. I felt I couldn't trust my eyes anymore. I shut my eyes for a long time to see if the creature would disappear. I didn't want to see him this morning. But when I opened my eyes he was still there, only now a few steps nearer, and his smell was strong around me.

"I'm lost, Big Foot," I said, speaking to him as though I thought he might understand me. "And if you let that McMurtry man see you, you'll be lost, too. So why don't you just disappear? That would make everything easier."

He made an odd little sound, as if he'd made a decision, because he covered the distance between us in two strides. I reached out and touched his hair. It was coarse and springy. Again the creature made that strange little cry as he sprang away from my touch. He began walking away.

I watched him from the boulder, but I didn't move. When I didn't follow, he stopped and looked back at me and made his sound, a little louder this time. "You want me to follow you?" I asked. I wasn't afraid of the creature, but I was a little leery of following him deeper into the woods. But after a second I shrugged and said, "What the heck? Take me to your leader."

He stayed well out in front of me, but not so far away that I couldn't keep up. After a little while, I began to notice a few familiar landmarks until finally I was back in my own part of the woods again. And now I had a new worry. What if McMurtry was in here somewhere with his gun and traps and nets? But what do you say to a Big Foot? Thank you very much. You've been a big help, but I know my way now. I didn't think he'd understand. Maybe if I just broke away and started through the woods on my own, he'd get the idea.

Though I didn't look back, I could hear the creature following me. Then suddenly I heard noise ahead of me as well. I looked nervously back over my shoulder to see if the Big Foot was still in sight the instant McMurtry stepped out of the trees in front of me.

"You're out early, kid," he said. "What's the matter?" His sharp eyes zeroed in on me. "Did you see him?"

"I haven't seen anybody but you."

"Something's making you look awfully skittish. And you're sort of overdressed for a stroll in the woods."

"I'm just taking a shortcut through here to home."

"Kid, you're a real mess. Now you'd best just tell me what's been going on." He reached toward me, but I jerked back away from him. He said, "I was just going to get the leaves out of your hair. Did you sleep in the woods last night?"

"What if I did?" I said. I was too tired and hungry to think up a lie. All I wanted was to get home before Dad missed me.

"You got spunk, kid. Not many would want to share a bed with Big Foot."

"There's no Big Foot in this woods," I said, but I knew he wouldn't believe me. He saw the truth in my eyes. When I told Dad the truth he wouldn't believe me, and when I told this man a lie he wouldn't believe me. I was batting a thousand.

"Whatever you say, kid." The lines of McMurtry's face tightened, and a strange, cold look came into his eyes. "Where's your dog, kid? I wouldn't have thought you'd be out here without him."

The look on his face scared me more than seeing the Big Foot had ever scared me. I didn't answer him but began moving away from him toward home. I didn't dare look over my shoulder again. I could only hope the creature had made himself scarce.

McMurtry put his hand on my shoulder and stopped me. When I tried to shake him off, he tightened his grip until pain shot down my arm. "Let go of me," I said.

"Sure, kid," he said. "In a minute. First you've got to listen to me and listen good. I'm getting old, and before I get too old, I'm going to take me a Big Foot. And you're going to help me."

"Never."

"I think you will," he said and grinned. "I told you your dog was too trusting."

It took me a minute to realize what he meant, but then I wanted to kill him. "What have you done with Maybe?" I screamed.

"Don't worry, kid. He's all right. And he'll stay all right if you help me catch your Big Foot."

I lowered my head and charged him. He was bigger and stronger, but not nearly as quick as I was, and my shoulder hit him right in the midriff. He went down with a whoosh of breath. His gun flew away from him and went off as it hit the ground. The sound echoed through the trees as I lunged for his shoulders to pin him down. But he rolled away from me and somehow came up with his rifle pointed straight at my chest.

His mouth moved but made no sound as he struggled to catch his breath. I eased back from the gun. Fear mixed with my rage until I thought my heart would explode.

"What's going on here?" a voice demanded behind me.

Chapter Twelve

I tore my eyes away from the gun barrel to look behind me. "Dad!" I said.

Dad's eyes were fastened on McMurtry, who seemed to shrink to an even smaller size there in front of Dad. "Put that gun down," Dad ordered. His voice was cold and hard.

"Sure thing." McMurtry had finally caught his breath. He laid the gun down and then said, "The boy here just attacked me. I had to defend myself."

"With a gun?" Contempt leaked out around every word. Dad looked over at me for the first time. "Are you all right, Shane?" Dad's face was gray and drawn in harsh lines. Two scratches that were still bleeding stood out on his cheek.

I nodded.

"Then let's get out of here," Dad said.

"I can't," I said, finding my voice again.

"I know what happened last night," he said. He raised his hand from his side as though he wanted to reach toward me, but then he let it fall back.

"You do? I hadn't wanted him to know. I had wanted just to tuck it all back inside the dark place in my mind and cover it up again.

"Jackie called me. I've been looking for you since daylight."

Tears came to my eyes. "I tried to come home, Dad. Really I did, but I couldn't find my way in the dark."

"It's all right, son," Dad said and reached out for me. I couldn't remember the last time we had hugged. There had been lots of slaps and affectionate punches but no real hugs. Dad's voice sounded strange and thick as he said again, "Let's go home."

I pulled back. "I can't, Dad." When I saw the look on his face, I hurried on. "It's not that. It's him. McMurtry. He's got Maybe."

Dad looked as if he didn't understand. "Was Maybe at home?" I asked. It could be that McMurtry was bluffing.

Dad shook his head slowly. "I called for him this morning, but he didn't come. I figured he'd found you in the woods."

My hopes fell. "He's got him."

Dad turned back to McMurtry, who had scrambled to his feet and was now leaning against a tree watching us. Under his cap his eyes were narrow and wary, and he had a firm grip on the gun.

"I think I'd better find out what's going on here," Dad said.

The little man's hand tightened on the gun, and he raised it the slightest bit. Still, when he spoke it was casually, as though Dad had asked about the weather. "Well, it's like the kid said. I've got his dog, but I ain't going to do the mutt no harm. No, sir, not as long as I get what I want."

"And what could you possibly want from my son?" I was standing close enough to Dad to feel the tremble of fury run through him.

McMurtry spat on the ground before he said, "All the kid has to do is lead me to the Big Foot and then I'll let his dog go."

"Big Foot?" Dad turned some of his fury on me.

"He read the story in the paper, Dad," I said quickly. "I told him it was just legends, that I haven't seen any kind of creatures, but he won't believe me."

"My son couldn't lead you to a Big Foot. There are no such creatures," he said.

"Oh, but you're wrong there, Buckley."

Dad's eyes narrowed at the use of his name.

McMurtry went on. "There are plenty of the creatures around, and your kid has seen one, maybe even struck up a friendship with him, or I miss my guess. Some folks have a feeling for the creatures, and the creatures know it."

"My son has not seen any creatures. He just told you that."

"There ain't no reason for you to get mixed up in this, Mr. Buckley. Me and the boy can work it out."

"How? By holding a gun on him and stealing his dog?"

McMurtry must have sensed that Dad was close to losing control, because he raised the gun another couple of inches. He said, "All the kid has to do is show me where he saw the Big Foot and tell me about it. Most folks are glad enough to tell their story to somebody who will believe them, but your kid's a little different from most."

Dad flinched. He didn't like hearing what he already feared put in words. "Your game's up, mister. Either the dog's home in an hour, or I call in the sheriff."

He put his arm around my shoulders and turned me away from the man. But McMurtry had the last word. He laughed and said, "If you think the sheriff is going to come in here after me, you're crazy. And even if he was fool enough to try, I can disappear almost as good as the Big Foot. You can ask your kid how good that is."

We didn't say anything all the way out of the woods. Dad let me lead the way. I wondered how many times he'd been lost while he was searching for me, but I didn't ask. He had searched for me. He had known where I was and why. He had found me.

At the house, I called for Maybe and whistled. The sound hung in the air, the most lonesome sound I'd ever heard.

"He'll let him go," Dad said and tightened his arm on my shoulders.

I didn't say anything, but I didn't believe it.

"Go clean up," Dad said. "I'll fix us something to eat after I call Josephine."

I heard him dial the phone as I climbed the stairs, and I felt awful because I'd worried Aunt Jo. I could imagine her sitting all night in her rocker by the phone waiting to know I was all right. The guilt was piling up in heavy loads on me. Everything was my fault. McMurtry in the woods. Maybe gone. The Big Foot in danger of being captured. Even Mom. But I couldn't think about that now. That was one door still closed in my mind. I wasn't sure I could stand it being wrenched open right now.

I stayed in the bathroom so long that Dad finally yelled at me from the bottom of the stairs. I dressed then and went down.

I could smell the pancakes before I got halfway down the stairs. Dad hadn't made pancakes since Christmas. It was sort of a tradition then.

"I hope you're hungry," Dad said as I came to the table.

"Starved," I said. But after the first few bites had taken the edge off my hunger, I couldn't eat any more. I was too worried about Maybe and about the questions in Dad's eyes. I was afraid to look at him. Afraid I'd see the frown there and that if I did, I might cry because now I knew why it was there.

I pushed my plate away and said, "I'm sorry about making you and Aunt Jo worry. I just couldn't think straight."

"I should have talked to you about it a long time ago. Josephine wanted me to, said she'd do it for me, but I didn't want you to have to know." Dad's voice sort of faded out.

I looked over at him, not meeting his eyes. He'd pushed his own plate away without touching his pile of pancakes.

Dad stared at the wall over my head. "I mean, it was bad enough her being gone." This time the silence came into the room to trap us both in our thoughts. After a long time Dad said, "I didn't want you to think that she wanted to leave us."

What else could I think, I wanted to yell out, but I didn't. I just sat silently and drew patterns in the syrup on my plate.

"She didn't, you know. Or she wouldn't have if she hadn't been sick."

The door in my own head began easing open, but I jammed a foot against it.

"I wouldn't see it," Dad said. I felt his eyes on me, and I pulled my own eyes up to meet his. The pain there made me drop my eyes back down as he kept talking. "I wouldn't admit how bad it was. I thought she would get better. Even the doctors said she just needed time."

"But she didn't want any more time," I said. My voice surprised me, coming out like that in the air between us.

"Yes, she did. Or she would have if she hadn't been sick." Dad reached across the table and took my hand. "She didn't aim to kill herself. I know she didn't. She just forgot how many pills she'd taken. She didn't aim to die. She just wanted to get away for a while."

I wanted to believe him, but I wasn't sure that I could. Not now. Not after last night when I had been forced to remember so much. Now I wanted to jerk my hand away from his and run again. It didn't matter where. Just to run and leave this all behind.

He took his hand away. "Anyway, I couldn't stand you hearing what people were saying even when they were trying to be kind. Then you kept having those dreams and seeing her." Dad was quiet for a minute before he said, "I knew we had to get away from there and start a whole new life."

Dad had tried to hide me from the truth, and in its way it had worked. I had hidden away the memories of my mother's death, but they had been there all the time, sometimes pushing and shoving to get out. But I'd been afraid to remember. Suddenly the door in my mind burst open, and the ugly truth I'd been hiding from all these years flooded out into the open. It was my fault that my mother was dead! If I had called for help that day when I couldn't wake her up instead of waiting for Dad to get home, she might have lived. *It was my fault.*

As if Dad had read my mind he said, "If only I hadn't stayed at practice so late that night. I've beaten myself with that thought for years."

There was a terrible silence. Finally, Dad began again. "And then last night, I thought maybe I'd lost you, and I couldn't do anything. I couldn't look for you in the woods in the dark. I got lost a dozen times this morning in broad daylight. I have tried so hard to do the right things. I thought I was doing what had to be done to keep you safe, and then you weren't and it was my fault again." He turned away from me.

"Dad," I said and touched his shoulder. "Dad. It wasn't our fault."

It wasn't until he turned to hug me that I realized he was crying. "No, Shane," he said when he could find his voice. "It wasn't our fault."

Chapter Thirteen

I was glad to have the chore of clearing off the table. It put some of the ordinary back in the day. Then as I scraped the uneaten pancakes into the garbage pail, I remembered Maybe. Dad, too, must have been thinking about Maybe because he said, "I'm going to call the sheriff."

"He wouldn't be able to find Maybe," I said. "Even if he tried. You don't really think he'd send out a search team for a dog."

"He'll have to go after that man, McMurtry. I'm going to press charges against him."

"Dad," I said and waited until he looked at me. "I have to go hunt for Maybe."

"You can't go back in there with that man on the loose. He has a gun, don't forget," Dad said. I knew he was seeing again the scene he had walked up on with me staring down the barrel of McMurtry's rifle.

"If Maybe's in the woods, I can find him. I know I can."

"Wanting to do something and being able to do it are two different things," Dad said, but he hadn't said no.

"I have to try."

He nodded and said, "I'll go with you."

"I can make better time on my own. Please, Dad. I'll be all right. I won't let McMurtry see me."

He hesitated between yes and no, and I took advantage of his moment of indecision. "Thanks, Dad. I'll be careful," I said as I escaped out the door before he could stop me.

Behind me Dad called something about the sheriff, but I didn't stop.

For all my confidence, I didn't know where to begin once I was in the woods. I really didn't know much about McMurtry. He could have come from any direction. My only hope of finding him was that Maybe would be barking because he was being kept captive. So I walked and then I stopped and listened for a long time.

It seemed like hours before I finally heard the sound I'd been listening for. I cut straight through the trees toward Maybe. When I got close, I placed my feet carefully so not a leaf rustled as I crept up on the spot.

Maybe caught my scent and strained so against the chain that held him to a tree that his barks came out in high, squeaky yelps. I could only hope McMurtry was out hunting the Big Foot as I moved out of the cover of the trees to free Maybe. I should have known McMurtry would be waiting for me.

"It took you long enough, boy," he said behind me. "I thought you'd be back an hour ago."

I whirled to face McMurtry, who had his gun looped in the crook of his arm with the barrel pointed toward the ground, but I knew he could pull it up in an instant. I tried to make my voice calm and firm as I said, "I've come for my dog."

"And you can have him, too. I've decided I don't want any go arounds with the local law. Or your dad, either." He looked around. "Where is he? I wouldn't think he'd let you back in here without him today."

"He's coming. With the sheriff and his men." I didn't doubt that was true. I just wasn't sure they'd be able to find me when they did come.

"Well, that's okay. We'll be through with our little piece of business long before they get here, or I miss my guess. Matter of fact, I'm glad your father ain't with you. He's one of the doubters. I could tell that easy enough. Is that why you don't want to tell about seeing the creature?"

"I haven't seen a creature," I said. I kept my voice low and controlled. With enough practice I might make a good liar.

"That's what your mouth says, but your eyes don't lie hardly so good, kid."

"I want my dog." I turned away from him and went toward Maybe again. Maybe was wriggling all over, with his ears cocked up as if to ask what took me so long. I was within arm's reach of Maybe's head before McMurtry fired at the ground in front of me. Dirt kicked up on my shoes, and I couldn't keep from jumping back. Maybe cowered on the ground.

"You can't have him yet," McMurtry said, shifting the balance of his body over to his other foot. "Not until we finish our business."

"We haven't got any business together." My voice wasn't quite so calm now.

"You tell me about the Big Foot. Everything about the Big Foot."

"There's nothing to tell."

He raised his gun and pointed it toward Maybe. "I'd hate to have to shoot your mutt."

"You're crazy," I said. I really didn't think he would shoot Maybe. It seemed so senseless.

"Maybe so," McMurtry said as he squeezed the trigger. The bullet whizzed over Maybe's back just a few inches from its mark. McMurtry waited until the sound died away before he went on. "But I don't intend leaving here without finding out what I came to find out. Now, you're going to tell me or the next bullet will be lower. I've never liked dogs, you know." He lowered the barrel of the gun.

I believed him now, and I grabbed at words desperately. "All right. All right. What do you want to know?" I asked. I searched my mind for a way to stop him. Still I couldn't tell the truth. Now even now, with Maybe's life depending on it. At least not yet, not until I tried everything else. My Big Foot deserved that much.

I took a quick look around at the woods and had the feeling that he was there watching.

"You think he's out there right now, don't you?" McMurtry said. His eyes were sharp and piercing as they swept the woods after mine.

"I don't know," I said.

"But you have seen him." The man could hardly contain his excitement.

I edged a little closer to Maybe, but McMurtry raised his gun again and stopped me. "All right!" I screamed. "I'll tell you! He was six or seven feet tall, or he might have been when he was upright. When I saw him he was hunched over, using his arms for walking. He had brown hair."

"His face?" McMurtry prompted. "What did his face look like?"

"I don't know. It was sort of hairy, and it seemed as if his eyes were black. I didn't get a really good look at him."

"You're lying," McMurtry said.

"No, no. It's true, and now that I've told you, you have to let Maybe go." I moved a step or two closer until I could touch Maybe's brown fur. Maybe whimpered and quivered all over. "It's all right," I whispered. "It's going to be all right."

"You're lying to me, kid. Everything you've said has been a lie." McMurtry raised the gun back up.

I moved between Maybe and the gun. My back felt as if it was naked with ice pellets pounding into it as I unfastened Maybe's collar. I looked over my shoulder at McMurtry. "You wanted me to tell you something. Okay, I told you. Now let us go."

"I ought to shoot the both of you. By the time they found you out here, I'd be long gone."

"You might shoot dogs," I said as I pulled the collar loose from around Maybe's neck. "But you wouldn't shoot me." Maybe was free, but he wouldn't run away without me.

"I wouldn't be too sure, kid," McMurtry said. "You've caused me a heap of trouble and wasted a week or more of my time."

"I never said I'd seen a Big Foot. That was all your idea."

I slapped Maybe on the rear, and we took off in a run. A spatter of shots rang out behind us and thudded into the ground and the trees. A sharp, piercing pain bit into my upper arm, and a moment later Maybe yelped and dropped.

"I could have killed you, kid," McMurtry hollered after me. "Now you come back here and talk to me straight."

I didn't bother to answer him. I was kneeling over Maybe, who whimpered and tried to lick my hand. He'd taken the bullet in his hindquarters, and though he tried to get up when I asked him to, he couldn't. I smoothed his ears back and talked to him. "Poor old dog. This Big Foot business hasn't been any fun for you."

Then, without looking back at McMurtry, I put my arms under Maybe's body and lifted him up. My arm stung, but I was only grazed. I stood up. My knees wobbled under Maybe's weight, but after a few steps I found my stride. It would be a long walk out of the woods.

I glanced back once at McMurtry. He was watching me with his gun sighted. After a moment he said,

"You should have told me the truth, kid. Then I wouldn't have shot your dog. You should have helped me. We could have both been famous."

"The only strange creature in Chance Woods is you," I said. If the earth had opened and swallowed him up, I wouldn't have so much as reached down a hand to help him. I began moving again with Maybe. I had to get him to a vet. When I looked around again the little man was gone, and again I thought of trolls and dwarfs.

I met Dad and the sheriff and a couple of deputies before I had gone very far. They had heard the shots and that guided them to me. Dad helped me get Maybe to a vet, but the sheriff and his men stayed in the woods looking for McMurtry. They found no sign of him. He had disappeared as eerily as he had appeared. Of course, they found no sign of a Big Foot either.

The vet said Maybe would be all right, but that he'd always have a limp and be stiff in cool weather. That, too, would be my fault.

I told Jackie as much the next day when she rode her bike out to the house.

"That's nonsense," she said in her matter-of-fact voice. I thought it must be nice to be so sure about everything, but then maybe she wasn't. Maybe she only sounded that way.

"I wrote the article about Big Foot."

"Then I could be at fault more than you. You didn't want it to be in the *Brookfield News*. I was the one who told Mrs. Smith she could submit it. Are you going to blame me for a crazy old man coming along and believing all that nonsense?''

"No," I said with a grin.

"Good," she said briskly. She swept her dark hair back into a ponytail and then let it fall back on her shoulders. She picked a piece of lint off her blue jeans. Finally she said, "I'm sorry about the other night, Shane."

"I guess I'm the one who should be sorry," I said. "I just couldn't talk right then. I'm not sure I can talk about it now."

"That's okay," she said. "But also I'm sorry that the party didn't work out for you."

When I looked up with a questioning frown, she went on. "Oh, you know. So that you could get to know Tami better, and all that."

"I didn't go to the party to get to know Tami better," I said. I rubbed Maybe's fur; he was lying between us on the porch. "The only reason I went was so I could try to talk to you. To apologize so you wouldn't be mad at me."

"I wasn't really mad." When I looked up at her, she added, "Well, maybe a little, but only for a while."

"A while? You wouldn't even eat Friday because you didn't want to take the chance of seeing me."

"That's not true," Jackie insisted, but then she grinned. "I just wasn't hungry."

We both knew she was lying, but it was all right. I felt as if I could tell her anything, even about my mother, and she would understand. But there would be other times. Right then I didn't want to talk about Mama or the Big Foot or McMurtry. I said, "I'm going away to camp in a week. Dad got me this job. I'm going to be a counselor, but I'll get to come home sometimes on weekends.''

"Good," she said. "I'd like to come over sometimes and make sure Maybe's all right."

"That's the only reason?"

She smiled before looking away at the woods. "Are you afraid to go into the woods today after all that's happened?"

"No," I said.

"Weren't you afraid while you were lost?"

"I felt awfully alone, but I don't know that I was afraid. Would you like to take a walk there today?"

"Yes," she said.

I didn't take Jackie to my special place by the creek. Perhaps someday I would, but not yet.

We didn't see the Big Foot that day or any of the other days we walked in the woods. Somehow I didn't expect to. He'd been a gentle creature who McMurtry had frightened back into total hiding with his gun.

Sometimes I wonder if I ever really saw the creature at all, or if maybe it was all my imagination as Dad thinks to this day. Then I remember the photos stuck in between the wall and the shelf in my closet.

One shows half of a Big Foot print. The second is the one I took when I met the Big Foot face-to-face. The photo is dim, but the shape of the creature is unmistakable. The last photo is the bonus. The day I missed the shot of the squirrel I captured the image of a much larger creature lurking in the background. It couldn't possibly be explained away by talk of shadows and such. Even the strange tilt of his head is obvious as he stares toward me, and I wonder how it was I hadn't noticed him when I snapped the shutter.

Once or twice I've been tempted to show Dad the pictures, but we don't talk about the Big Foot. Ever. We do sometimes talk about Mama now. Both the good times and the bad. And Dad took the coaching job at school, so now there's always sports talk at the table at night. I held my breath until I found out he doesn't expect me to play. I'm still training for the cross-country team. The more I run, the more I like it. My speed is increasing but not enough to win any races this season. But I'll finish. I'll always finish. Dad is beginning to understand that.

I keep the photographs hidden. Life's simpler that way. But sometimes I take them out to look at them, and sometimes I leave an apple by the creek.

Delivered right to your door will be heart-felt romance novels by the finest authors in the field, including Diana Palmer, Brittany Young, Rita Rainville, and many others.

You will also get absolutely FREE, a copy of the Silhouette Books Newsletter with every shipment. Each lively issue is filled with news about upcoming books, interviews with your favorite authors, even their favorite recipes.

When you take advantage of this offer, you'll be sure not to miss a single one of the wonderful reading adventures only Silhouette Romance novels can provide.

To get your 4 FREE books, fill out and return the coupon today!

This offer not available in Canada.

Silhouette ❀ *Romance*®

Silhouette Books, 120 Brighton Rd., P.O. Box 5084, Clifton, NJ 07015-5084